PRAISE FOR
THE BLACK DRAGON
BOOK 1 OF THE MYSTERIUM TRILOGY

"A laudable and likable hero. The unusual location, intriguing characters, and a fast-paced plot further set this series opener apart. A clever mashup of crime drama and magical realism makes for an auspicious series start."
—*Kirkus Reviews*

"This first installment in the Mysterium series is filled with action and stage magic, though Danny's struggles with identity and his parents' deaths are never far from the surface, making this adventure more than gangster brawls and misdirection."
—*Booklist*

"Gripping series introduction . . . . The pacing is fast, featuring a strong blend of intense action and inner struggle. The ending is powerful and thrilling."
—*School Library Journal*

MYSTERIUM **2**

THE PALACE OF MEMORY

JULIAN SEDGWICK

CAROLRHODA BOOKS
Minneapolis

First American edition published in 2017 by Carolrhoda Books

Text copyright © Julian Sedgwick, 2014
First published in Great Britain in 2014 by Hodder Children's Books, a division of
Hachette Children's Books, an Hatchette UK company

Cover illustration by Patricia Moffett
Cover illustration copyright © 2017 by Lerner Publishing Group, Inc.

Carolrhoda Books
A division of Lerner Publishing Group, Inc.
241 First Avenue North
Minneapolis, MN 55401 USA

For reading levels and more information, look up this title at www.lernerbooks.com.

Map, skull, and code charts © Laura Westlund/Independent Picture Service.

Main body text set in Bembo Std 12.5/17.
Typeface provided by Monotype Typography.

Library of Congress Cataloging-in-Publication Data

The Cataloging-in-Publication Data for *The Palace of Memory* is on file at the Library
of Congress.
ISBN 978-1-4677-7568-7 (trade hardcover)
ISBN 978-1-5124-2690-8 (eb pdf)

LC record available at https://lccn.loc.gov/2016008432

Manufactured in the United States of America
1-37418-18416-4/13/2016

FOR ISABEL
2707 13616 0712

PROLOGUE

The body will still be warm. She knows that.

She knows because she was the one to close the man's eyes. Because it was her hands that stuffed his body into the antique fairground ride. Because it was she—La Loca—who fired the three silenced shots that killed him.

Pwoomph, pwoomph, pwoomph—the stuffing kicked out of his down-filled parka, his eyes surprised, then horror-struck, then glazing over. Caught up in something much bigger than his own pathetic world of pickpocketing and petty crime, she thinks. But that's life: wrong place, wrong time, end of story.

As she waits in the shadows, she knows precisely when the staff will come to open the bloodred airplane ride and discover the body, knows every step of her escape, how long it will be until rigor mortis comes to lock the young man tight. She knows because she's seen it so many times before. Because she's a professional, meticulously planning the hours, minutes, seconds that lead up to the death. And the ones that come after.

Far below, Barcelona lies spread in pale November sunshine, its buildings jammed against the blue wall of the Mediterranean beyond. Her eyes fasten on the tall, dreamlike spires of the Sagrada Familia cathedral, the yellow cranes spidering up, hanging over its perpetual, slow-motion construction. It's taken them a hundred years already, and still they keep building. And people call *her* crazy!

Still that smell's hanging around her: the back-of-the-throat stench from when she burned the forty-nine dot pattern onto the dead man's back with the cigarette. Well, if that's what the clients want, then that's what they get. And it's given her the chance to take care of some other business too—plant some evidence to throw off the police and get rid of a potential problem with her accomplice.

She takes a matchbox from her pocket, glances at the fierce tiger prowling on its label, and places it in the gloom next to the discarded cigarette packet.

The woman takes her leave then, dropping down a forgotten path out of the fairground, her lime-green coat knifing through the twisty pines and cacti back toward the city. As she goes, she pulls the victim's mobile from her pocket. With gloved hands she plucks out its heart and brain—the battery and SIM—and chucks them away amongst the fallen, dead leaves.

ACT ONE

MEMORY IS THE TREASURE HOUSE
AND GUARDIAN OF ALL THINGS.

—*Cicero*

1

WHY THE CIRCUS
WAITS FOR NO ONE

Thirty-six hours later.

Danny is on his own, running headlong through the darkened backstreets of Paris. His feet are light, fast on the pavement, his backpack thumping against his back as he races toward the River Seine.

He stops for a moment, his breath thickening the cold air as he peers into the night, checking the next corner for trouble, for dark shadows smudged in the recesses away from the streetlights, eyes and ears straining, heart pounding. *Got to be careful. Maybe they already know where I am? But how could they?*

He glances at his watch. Five minutes. Five precious minutes left to catch the night train to Barcelona.

Can't miss it. What would I do then? Sneak back to the hotel with my tail between my legs? Wait for the morning and be picked up by the police—and then have to argue and plead with Aunt Laura? Wouldn't work. It's not an option.

A voice from the past is whispering in his ear—Rosa, the Mysterium's ringmistress—cajoling the company on some long-forgotten, long-distance journey: *Faster, pussycats, faster! The circus won't wait for anyone!* The memory gives him new strength, and he's already running again, senses so alert that he smells the cold, dark river before he sees it.

He has no ticket. Hardly any money—just the forty euros he has "borrowed" from Laura. Any tiredness Danny has felt has been flushed from his system now by a rush of anxiety and urgency. He thinks of his aunt, asleep in the hotel, numbed by jetlag at the end of their first stopover day in Paris. What will Laura do when she wakes up and finds out? Alert the authorities? Or force Major Zamora to bring him back straightaway? *Just got to hope the note will buy me enough time,* he thinks, *hope that Laura will have the confidence to let me have my own way—for a few days at least. Hope my own confidence holds out. I can do it—at least I think I can. After all, I'll be with Zamora.*

And besides, something else is balancing his nerves, making his feet strike the pavement just that much harder: if only briefly—maybe "for just one weird, beautiful night only!"—he will be reentering the Mysterium, stepping back through the magic portal of the curtain, into a world he thought was gone forever. A smile jumps across his face.

I'm running away to join the circus! Or re-join it, more like. Once he could even have said he was going home—but, of course, that's not true anymore. Without Dad, without Mum, what will the Mysterium be? Certainly not the place he knew and loved, but something damaged, sadder, older . . .

The smile is gone.

Keep focused, dummy, he thinks to himself. *One lock at a time.* He's back on the trail of the Forty Nine, rushing to warn Zamora—maybe save his life. That's enough for now. At least he feels strong again and ready for whatever is about to happen. Running, yes. But for the first time in weeks, months—years—he's running *toward* the trouble, not away from it.

Eyes narrowing in determination, as if taking aim at a distant target, he sprints for the night train.

2

WHY SOME GIRLS
DON'T SAY GOOD-BYE

Back in Hong Kong—after the battle on the hijacked cargo boat, the triumphant return to harbor—Danny had started to wonder if he would ever feel normal again. Reeling from the blows, the constant ebb and flow of adrenaline, his body and mind had taken their time to recover.

He lay in his room at the Pearl Hotel, drifting in and out of delayed concussion and shock. Dreams blurred against memories of the darkening sea, his fight for life. In one confused moment, seemingly awake, he thought Dad was in the room, crouched at his bedside trying to help him out of a straightjacket, voice pitched to the low rumble he used when beckoning Danny into a secret. But not one single word was distinct. And then there was Mum too! Stepping lightly, eyes fixed on an invisible *point de mire*—anchor point—wire—walking her way through the air over his head into nothing. To who knows where.

"Mum!"

He sat bolt upright in bed, hand reaching out into the gloom for the spectral figures—but they were gone, the room empty and silent but for the never-ending sigh of the air-conditioning, and he slumped back down and closed his eyes.

Zamora, Sing Sing, Aunt Laura—even Inspector Ricard—took turns keeping him company those first few days. Laura pacing the room like an animal cooped in too small a cage. Zamora gazing out at the harbor, his short, bowed legs planted firmly. Ricard thoughtful in the armchair, long fingers steepled under his chin.

Or they gathered in twos or threes at the foot of his bed, whispering quick conversations, believing him to be asleep. Fragments filtered down into Danny's awareness. Words that made no sense and yet tugged at him, desperate for attention.

Zamora to Sing Sing: ". . . well, call me when you know for sure. I'll talk to the others. *Pero*, I can't promise anything . . ."

Sing Sing to Zamora: "But you can *ask*. Do that at least for me!"

Zamora to Laura: ". . . thing is I don't want to upset the lad now. You'll have to tell him."

To which Laura replied in a fierce whisper, "Well, thanks a lot! Look, our first priority is the protection routine."

Danny rolled away under the duvet, like a swimmer turning at the end of a length, catching a snatch of conversation, then curling back into the confusion of the water. There would be time enough to find out more. For now, he just had to keep swimming. Avoid sinking. Avoid drowning.

But three days after the escape, he was woken by Zamora shaking him firmly by the shoulder. The curtains were open, evening falling blue across Hong Kong, and the neon lights stacked around the harbor glowed against low, suffocating clouds.

"Wake up. Mister Danny! I've got to go, *amigo*." Danny struggled to understand.

"Go? Go where?"

"I've got to catch a plane. Got an important meeting back home—Barcelona. Good old Catalonia!"

"I need to talk to you, Major . . ." Danny tried

to rub the sleep from his eyelids, blinking, trying to make sense of things.

"There'll be time enough soon," the dwarf said, doing his best to reassure. "I waited as long as I could, to make sure you're A-OK." He smiled. "I'm going to get high-tech at last. We can do that Skype stuff."

"I . . . I . . ." Danny fumbled for the right words, but his head felt so fogged he couldn't find them.

"Must go, *amigo*. Taxi's waiting. I'd be letting people down, and you know how I hate to do that."

"But—"

"You get rested. Recovered. Then we'll talk. *Adios*, my friend."

Zamora turned away, his busy stride taking him to the door. But halfway he stopped and looked back, a genuine smile bursting across his face.

"*Carajo*! They didn't stand a chance against us, eh?!" And with that he was gone.

"Major!"

Danny tried to get to his feet, but his legs were tangled, unresponsive in the thick duvet. With an effort he sat up groggily on the edge of the bed, trying to summon extra reserves, desperate to call the Major back.

A sharp knock at the door stopped him mid effort. Zamora returning, perhaps?

"Yes?"

But the door opened to reveal Inspector Ricard. The Interpol man looked refreshed, his white suit as immaculate as ever, but concern deepened the lines on his long face.

"Don't try and get up yet, Danny," he said. "You need another day's rest at least. And we have to talk."

"I need to talk to Zamora—"

"First things first, *mon ami*. And Zamora's gone." And forensically, point by point, Ricard went through every detail about Kwan, the kidnapping, the Black Dragon. He listened intently to Danny's answers, making pages and pages of notes before finally puffing out his cheeks in resignation.

"I don't know. This may be the end of it. So far I can find no trail leading to any real organization beyond Kwan and the Dragon itself."

"But why did Kwan say that *his* boss wanted me dead?"

"Maybe you misunderstood? Stress and so on . . ."

"And what about the forty-nine dots at school?"

"Must have been the Black Dragon already stalking you. Maybe trying to warn Laura off?"

"And why copycat Dad's failed escape?"

"Sick joke? *Je ne sais pas.*"

"Couldn't you tell me more about Dad?" Danny asked, hungry for any new information that would make sense of the chaos enfolding him. "About the work he did for you?"

Ricard spread his hands in apology and shrugged. "As I said, Danny, I really wish I could—but I can't." *Fine! So I'll keep my secret too*, Danny thought: that image of the unidentified Khaos Klown watching Dad floundering from the smashed-up water torture cell, the flash of crimson paint that shouted sabotage. *I'll find out more first. Make sure I'm right, then tell Ricard. Or trade my hard-won info for his.*

"You have my card, Danny. Call me anytime, day or night." Ricard got up to leave. "And please do what your aunt says? I know how headstrong your dad could be. Your mum too! I think we can assume it runs in the family . . . ?"

Danny nodded. *You bet your life it does.*

If he felt disappointment at Zamora's departure, Danny felt crushed when, two days later, he found out that Sing Sing had also left abruptly, dissolving into the city without warning. Without a proper good-bye, even!

They had talked a bit about kung fu, circus skills, but any attempt Danny made to probe into his new friend's childhood—the loss of her own parents—was met with either bad jokes or long, heavy silences.

He had tried one last time, peering deeply into her eyes: "I'm really sorry about Charlie. I feel like I'm partly to blame. Don't you have any other family?"

"Nope. All gone," she said, forcing her voice to sound light, but Danny could see the emotion clutch at her throat. "Past always catches up with people like Charlie."

"So tell me about your mum."

"No. Flipping. Point." Sing Sing said, emphasizing the full stops with a chopping of her hand, cutting off further questions.

Back off, Danny thought. *Don't want to chase away the first proper friend I've made in ages.* He looked into her dark, watchful eyes, the determination sparking there, and tried not to think about how much he would miss her when he returned to England. In his head a brief fantasy: he and Sing Sing living in the same city, going to the same school, the girl's strength and spirit always with him . . . How hard the good-bye would be.

Perhaps she sensed that too and decided to make things easier. The next day he found an envelope slipped under the hotel door, addressed: *To Mister Danny Woo.*

Inside there was a postcard, a picture of the Hong Kong Peak Tram and on the reverse in jumpy handwriting:

I don't like good-byes, so I am not saying good-bye. We'll meet again. But I have to go and sort business on the mainland now.

Sing Sing.

No phone number, no e-mail, no address.

First, Zamora, now Sing Sing. The sense of frustration built as Danny reread the card, willing it to tell him more. The important people in his life always seemed to be in a hurry to get away, to hide things from him for his own good . . .

Or maybe she just doesn't care about me, he thought, his spirits plunging further.

He padded over to the window and watched the

boats writing their indecipherable messages on the water, the postcard clutched tight in his fingers.

So much has happened here, he thought—*from waking up under the rain outside the Golden Bat to when my head broke the surface of the water and I took that desperate gulp of air. Something's changed—and I can't give up this feeling of being alive. Fully alive. No way am I going back to being numbed by shock and grief like I was at Ballstone. I want those good days again—when you wake up at first light and it's a spring morning and the air's thundering with birdsong or the buzz and rush of some new city and you think anything—yes, anything—is possible. I'm taking control of my life, and nobody's going to stop me. And even if I have to do it completely on my own, I'm going to pick up the trail of the Forty-Nine and keep following it until I find out what happened to Mum, to Dad. To me.*

When Laura came in to say good morning, he was already dressed, eyes burning for action.

"Zamora's gone. Sing Sing's gone. When are *we* going, Aunt Laura?"

"Just had the all-clear from the police. I thought

we might go via Paris. We could do with a break, and no one will know we're there—"

"Are you going to buy that iPad you were talking about?"

"In duty-free. Why?"

"There's stuff I need to do."

3

WHY THE HUNTER STALKED THE NIGHT

Danny watched as the Hong Kong skyline swung in the porthole, dark green hills shrunk rapidly by altitude, then obliterated by blinding cloud. Laura was already at work, alternately sucking her pencil and jotting in her reporter's pad.

She glanced at him. "Got to get the details down while they're fresh. You can't leave it to memory, you know. That has a habit of remaking things how it wants them to be."

But Danny was preoccupied with other things. "Do you know what Sing Sing's doing on the mainland?"

"Reckon you know her better than I do."

"I think she wanted to talk about things, about her past. But she *didn't* want to at the same time."

"That's often the way. Especially with painful stuff, right?"

"I heard the Major talking to her. Sounded like they were discussing something important."

"Hmm, I don't know," Laura said, eyes darting away just a little bit too quickly, sidestepping the truth.

Danny spotted that easily and decided to press. "And he said to you: 'You'll have to tell him.' Tell me what?"

"It's nothing. Really."

"You're not telling the truth, Aunt Laura. I can see that!"

Laura sighed. "Oh look! You mustn't be cross with Zamora, Danny. He just didn't want to get you upset—"

Danny threw up his hands. "But it *makes* me cross when people don't tell me what's going on. Especially if it involves *me*!"

"I know. You're not a little kid anymore, like you said. But—technically—you're still a minor in the eyes of the law, Daniel."

"*What's* going on?"

Laura looked him in the eyes, watching the high-altitude light playing off the colors—the electric flash of the green, the depth of the brown—the questioning, searching, restless energy.

"Well, I'm sure you'd find out pretty soon anyway. They're reforming the Mysterium, Danny. Zamora and Rosa and what's-his-face Blanco have been talking with the others. That's what the Major's doing in Barcelona. He's gone for rehearsals—"

For a moment Danny was so stunned he didn't know what to say. "But they can't! Not without me!" he stumbled. "I mean, not without Mum, not without Dad!"

"Zamora thought it might be too painful—"

"But this is worse. I have to be there." Surely Laura must understand that!

"*First,* we need to sort out a school, the police protection routine—"

"I'm part of the Mysterium—"

"They're all very fond of you, I know, Danny. But in the end you're not a proper member of the company, are you? I know you used to help out. I know how much it means to you—"

"But—" But always he'd imagined that one day he would be a full-fledged part of the Mysterium. If only he had a proper act ready.

"No arguing!" Laura snapped. "Not until we get

a final green light from Ricard and can be sure the Forty-Nine are no more than smoke and mirrors, just a bunch of triads messing around. I promised your dad. Your mum."

Danny opened his mouth, was about to go back at her—but he knew it was no use right now. And what could be done forty thousand feet over China?

The worst of it was this: Zamora's secrecy seemed to go against everything the Major had said to him on the long, cold evening of the funeral in Berlin. Danny remembered the endless choking snowfall, how he had to fight to hold onto his emotions, how he had to fight to pull his imagination away from picturing what Mum and Dad looked like in their coffins. "I'll always be there for you, Danny," Zamora had said. "Trust me."

But clearly Danny couldn't do that, not after this . . . *betrayal*!

There was no other word for it. He thumped the porthole and gazed down at the thickly wadded clouds below.

"So what are they calling the show?" he said, after a few minutes of brooding silence.

"*Mysterium Redux*. The Mysterium reborn, I guess. Like that Velvet Underground album—"

"Were they planning it a long time?"

"You'll have to ask them. But first, we're going to enjoy Paris. I bleeding well need it."

And suddenly Danny felt cramped, claustrophobic in the narrow metal tube of the aircraft, desperate for fresh air and wide-open space, to decide his own movements, impatient to be landed, to have access to the Internet and start to pick away at the new clues found in Hong Kong.

Ominous weather greeted them in Paris. Heavy blue clouds sent volleys of hailstones pinging off their taxi roof as they pulled up at their hotel opposite the Père Lachaise cemetery, its autumn colors blurred by the white hail. Laura took one look at the weather and grimaced.

"Sheesh. Let's stay in. Save sightseeing for tomorrow. Hope you're not too disappointed."

"No," Danny said quickly, relieved. "That's fine. Can I get the iPad out?"

"Of course. I'm going to crash for a bit."

Within minutes of unpacking, Laura was out cold, fully clothed, in an armchair. But any tiredness Danny had been feeling was swept away now, anger and impatience taking hold as he ripped open the iPad's packaging and fumbled the plug into the socket to charge. The thought of the Mysterium flickering back into life without him was still raw, driving his actions. He paced to the window.

Outside, the evening was deepening. Hail lay melting in the cemetery, and darkness came creeping around the trees and tombs, like slow black water spreading toward him. It stirred memories—all too vivid—of his near-drowning in the South China Sea, and he drew the curtains quickly.

Don't need to wait for the iPad to charge, he thought, picking it up and banging in the hotel's Wi-Fi password. His fingers darted across the screen, tapping out *Mysterium + Barcelona*. More than 960,000 results. He took a breath and then clicked on the top hit.

Instant recognition! A news story in Spanish showed a photo of Darko Blanco and Aki—the Japanese Khaos Klown—holding one of the Aerialisque twins aloft on the roof of an antiquated blue streetcar. The girl (Beatrice or Izzy, he could never be sure which twin was which) was gushing flame from her mouth in long, rolling orange plumes. The headline read: *En Barcelona El Mysterium respira de nuevo.* In Barcelona the Mysterium breathes again. He had enough Spanish in the bits and pieces he'd picked up from Zamora to translate that without too much trouble.

So it was true! And *nobody* had let him know! But it made sense, of course. Barcelona was the birthplace of the Mysterium: where Dad had met Zamora and Rosa, where the first small shows had taken place, where the others had come to audition and rehearse. It made sense—but *how* it hurt that they were there without him now.

He scanned on down the search results.

Another hit—the company's new site? He felt his heart beating faster and tapped the screen—and there were the beautiful letters of the single word *MYSTERIUM* glowing against the midnight-blue background. When he clicked that, a looped video appeared—Rosa, in her punked-up ringmistress outfit, doing the fish-swallowing routine, the tail of a large mackerel sticking from her mouth, her cheeks bulging and eyes wide open—and the words: "Dive into the world of Mysterium Redux." Above that were tabs for *Mysterium History, Merchandise, Videos,* and *New Show Coming Soon*—a decent enough Web site, he noted, with lots of pages and nothing "under construction." So the reunion wasn't a spur-of-the-moment thing—they'd been planning it for a while at least, that was clear. All that time he'd been rotting in Ballstone, they'd been e-mailing each other, designing Web sites, rehearsing!

Danny clicked the tab marked *Venue* and recognized the extraordinary image at once: there, full-screen, were the towers and cranes of the Sagrada Familia cathedral, its fingers reaching skyward like natural forms—twisting coral, maybe, or gigantic tree stumps. He remembered being there once—it was years ago—but still recalled Dad's enthusiasm for the building, the madness and beauty of it all. A hundred years to build—and still not finished. What a venue!

Danny's fingers hovered over the screen. Caught up in the excitement of his discovery, he had almost forgotten that sense of betrayal. Now it came back again. Should he find out more? Perhaps better, after all, to let things be—turn away and start to find a new life elsewhere. If he wasn't wanted there—if even Zamora hadn't let him in on the secret—then perhaps it was better to stop chasing the past at all, and let Laura and Ricard guide him to a new school, a new safe (but dull) life. Let the rest of them get on with this new version of the Mysterium and walk away.

No. No! He shook his head hard.

I belong in that story. I can reclaim my own part in it. And anyway, he thought, *the solution to the whole mystery of what happened to—to me!—must lie there with the company, if it's to be found anywhere.*

His fingers were moving again—as if his body had decided before his mind—instinct tapping out the words: *Forty-Nine + Barcelona.* If his heart was beating quickly before, now it was racing as his eyes flicked down the results.

Nothing obvious on the first couple of pages of results, just fragments of news stories: "Forty-nine illegal immigrants seized in Barcelona." "Messi scores goal number forty-nine for season."

What was the Spanish for forty-nine? *Cuarenta y nueve.* He thumped that into the search bar and hit return.

And up bloomed an image that stilled his fingers above the glowing surface of the tablet. Recognition and disbelief and fear all at once as he looked at the photo: a body lay crumpled—its head wrenched away as if in pain or denial of the situation—jammed into the doorway of an old-fashioned fairground ride, a chubby, red plane at the top of a flight of metal steps. The upper body bare in the photo flash. And dabbed on the man's exposed back was that now familiar forty-nine dot pattern.

Or at least something that looked distinctly like it. But it couldn't be, could it?

He stretched the image with his fingers, pushing his face close to the tablet—but, as he zoomed in, the pattern pixelated, the smudgy black marks as good as disappearing. Could that be a ring around a dot to the left—closer to the center than the others he'd seen before? Danny squinted, trying to resolve the blurred image, the blood coursing in his ears. How to be sure?

Quickly he ran his finger over the text—and there it was in the third paragraph: "*cuaranta y nueve puntos quemado en la espalda.*" *Puntos* had to be dots— like "points"—but what about the rest? A quick copy and paste into a translation site and he was faced with the words: "forty-nine dots burned onto his back."

He checked the date on the newspaper article: just three days ago. The danger had to be real. *Maybe it means that the target isn't just Mum and Dad—and me—but the whole company,* he thought. Zamora, per-haps! Or maybe it was the evidence he needed that someone in the Mysterium—presumably one of the Khaos Klowns—was in it up to the neck. *I need to get there. Right now . . .*

For a moment—brief, never serious—he thought about waking Laura and telling her about the image, but already he could hear her warding him off, saying they should leave things to Interpol and Inspector Ricard, to the experts.

Forget it!

In a fumble of hushed packing, Internet train checking, and note scribbling, he cast himself loose: slipping from the hotel room; down the empty back stairs; out of a fire escape; and away through an echoing, deserted garage.

Outside, the night had fallen and the temperature with it, hail-slush refreezing in the gutters and the street lighting doing little to lift the darkness radiating off the cemetery. He pulled the hood up on his black Mysterium Crew tracksuit top, took one glance back, and then melted away into the shadows. In the sky, just above the hushed trees and graves, the constellation of Orion stood balanced on one leg, a massive figure looming over the sleeping city.

The Hunter—poised, ready to strike.

4

WHY MONSTERS LURK
IN THE DEPTHS?

Faster, Pussycats!

And so Danny is charging full pelt into the train station, hearing Rosa's voice whispering again in his ear. It feels good to be running, both the fear and frustration eased by taking action.

The concourse of the Gare de'Austerlitz is awash with commuters and tourists. Platform announcements blur on the cold air. Hard to understand but he knows where he's heading—platform 4 and the Trenhotel. He weaves around family groups, slips past a police officer in the wake of a group of nuns. Best to be on the safe side, keep out of sight in case Laura has already woken and raised the alarm. In his pocket his phone is switched off. Can the police track it even then? Perhaps you have to take the battery out? *As long as I can get to Barcelona, I can convince Zamora that I should be there. And then, with his strength added to mine, anything will be possible.*

Two guards stand to either side of the barrier to platform 4, one checking the ticket of a flustered businessman, the other scanning the hall for late passengers. He has sharp eyes, a hawkish nose, the kind of face that says he will be resistant to any kind of hypnotic suggestion or emotional persuasion. *So time for distraction*, Danny thinks. Sometimes, if you don't want attention, it's best to make a lot of fuss, grab it all—and then throw it away at someone else.

He hurries his feet, taking his wallet from his pocket, then abruptly changes direction as if rushing after someone leaving a train from another platform.

"Hey!" he shouts as loudly as he can. "Excuse me, monsieur! You've dropped something!" Everything—his eyes, his arm, the extended wallet—is pointed with all his strength in the direction of an imaginary departing passenger. Both guards look up, their focus first pulled onto Danny and then bounced away toward his imaginary quarry. In that brief second he takes his chance. He spins, chops his stride, and vaults the disabled barrier, smoothly, almost without a sound, before sprinting down the platform and ducking into the first carriage. Seconds later, the departure alarm sounds and the doors hiss shut along the whole length of the night train.

Heart racing, he makes his way to the first toilet cubicle he can find and locks himself in. *So far so good. Lie low for ten or fifteen minutes to be on the safe side*, he thinks. *Then find a place to bed down and get some rest.*

But the plan is quickly thwarted. For the first hour or so, he's forced to play a game of hide-and-seek with the guard—the same sharp-eyed one from the ticket barrier.

The man is thorough, making several passages of the entire length of the sleeper, checking tickets, answering questions, snagging the people he missed the first time. All the while his quick eyes are peering around, checking the next part of the train car, looking for something—or someone. *Is he on to me?* Danny wonders. *Mustn't let him find me before Barcelona. Might get arrested or kicked off at some lonely station in the foothills of the Pyrenees. Or sent straight back to Paris.*

So first, he slips into an empty sleeper compartment, then from that to the toilet again, then back to the buffet, then—finally—when he hasn't seen the guard for a full fifteen minutes, he wriggles into a hidey-hole behind a hefty suitcase in a baggage compartment.

Danny pulls the hood up over his head and tries to get warm, comfortable, to gather his courage tightly around him. *Really on my own now*, he thinks. *At least until I reach Barcelona and find Zamora. But he should have told me about the reunion . . .*

The train sways, piling on the speed as it dashes south. One by one the other passengers must be going to their sleeping compartments. It would be cozy, this nighttime express, if the stakes weren't so high. He hears footsteps, laughter, half a dozen languages drifting past. Then the silences between the conversations get longer, and gradually the train falls asleep.

He's longing for some rest himself but can't risk being caught with his defenses down, so instead he concentrates on stretching one piece of himself at a time, trying to ward off the cramp and pins and needles. It reminds him of when, during a particular show—*Carnevil*—he had to hide for ten minutes bent double in a suitcase, ready for the big reveal of one of Dad's tricks.

To distract himself, he starts to run the whole show in his head, trying to recall the music cues, the lighting, the order of the acts. He sees Darko climbing a spotlit pole, pulling himself into death-defying balances as the thing swayed gently at first, then more and more violently, while Billy the guitarist shredded feedback from his smashed-up Telecaster. As the storm of applause subsided, like a ship's mast coming to rest on a calm sea, the pole stilled—and Darko stood, poised, scanning the horizon like a lookout.

Suddenly he produced a red flag and hurled it to the ground to start the demolition derby below, releasing the Khaos Klowns in their souped-up bumper cars, faces hidden behind the skull masks, sending choking flame and smoke up into the hemisphere.

The Klowns. That stops the flow of his thoughts.

So if it is a Klown, which one do I suspect? Try as he might, he can add no more to the memory—so hard-won—that had come to him as he escaped from the improvised water torture. Just that red smear on the pants of one of them, nothing to recall which of the Klowns was behind the mask.

What about Aki? A rebel, his face studded with piercings, the quick spark of humor in his eyes, the love of jokes and riddles. But a swift reaction if criticized that would send his stubby mohawk twitching, counterarguments flying, a sense of indignation revving him to full blast. What else? His left hand missing half the ring finger—disturbing but fascinating. "And keep clear if he's been at the drink," Dad used to say darkly.

Or Bjorn? The strongest of the three, an African orphan adopted by Swedish parents. Silent 90 percent of the time and intensely private, thoughtful. The safest catcher anyone had ever seen on the trapeze, people used to say. And yet even as a young boy, Danny had been aware that Bjorn had occasional volcanic eruptions of temper. He could never forget seeing Bjorn, fired to beyond boiling point by racist taunts from an outspoken roustabout, slowly forming his meaty hand into a fist and then punching it straight through the plywood wall of one of the caravans.

What about Joey? His spiky red hair as vibrant as his mind was quick. The best actor of the three, surefooted, a brilliant parkour runner in his spare time: free-running his way around whichever city they found themselves in, vaulting stairwells and running up concrete walls. A risk taker, with a heavy French accent that he exaggerated for effect and that sometimes hid what he was trying to say. A bit of a troublemaker, Rosa used to say, and liable to improvise a move mid-performance to "make it feeeeel reeeaaal," which occasionally led to accidents. The rumor also went that he had run with street gangs in his hometown of Montpellier and had spent time in a juvenile detention center. Perhaps that was when he'd gotten those big discolored areas of scarring on both forearms—burns, perhaps, or a car accident?

Danny shakes his head. Each of them lived on the edge for sure, but he can't imagine why *any* of them would have wanted to hurt Dad. Or Mum. And yet, in those last few years, he knew there was trouble in the company from time to time. It would set Dad and Darko—or Dad and Zamora—to whispered discussion, trying to defuse whatever was brewing in the caravans and trailers clustered around the circus tent.

Maybe there was far more to that trouble than I guessed. Wish I'd paid closer attention, he thinks. *I need to remember.*

It was Dad's belief that everything you had ever seen, heard, tasted, felt was laid down somewhere in your memory. Every single word and image and thought locked away inside a vast, dark labyrinth of filing cabinets and corridors and hidden rooms.

"Memory's a treasure house," he would say, "but the lights aren't always on. It's dark down there—and sometimes there are monsters prowling around in that darkness. Remember the Minotaur!"

But if you were brave enough, you could go down into those unlit chambers and shine a light around, and the things lurking in the shadows were suddenly brought blinking into the light.

So let's be brave, Danny thinks. *Keep pushing the memories, looking for anything that's been repressed or forgotten.*

He tries to make himself more comfortable, picking up the thread of that particular show. After the Klowns had been plucked from their wrecked chariots, transformed into white-winged angels in the arms of the Aerialisques, the music calmed. Billy put a cello bow to the shining blade of his musical saw. In fragile, bending notes, he picked out the melody: *Clair de Lune*. Moonlight.

And right on cue, a large crescent moon rose into the air, carrying Mum in her silver bodysuit, high up above the open-mouthed, upturned heads of the audience. A heart-stopping moment as she stepped from the moon onto the wire, and it shivered as it took her weight, her gaze suddenly one of absolute

focus. No safety line. She refused one most nights—
"Otherwise, Danny, it means *nothing*," she would
whisper.

He falls asleep now to that memory, rocked by
the train, knowing he is risking more than just a
little bit.

He is risking *everything*.

"Allez! Votre billet, monsieur!"

A hand is shaking him roughly by the shoulder,
and strong sunshine is raking his grainy, sleep-filled
eyes.

"Levez vous! Maintenant."

The sharp-eyed guard, his face creased by anger,
beckoning Danny from his hiding place.

"Vite!"

"I'm sorry," Danny says, struggling to his feet
from behind the big suitcase—but his right leg has
gone to sleep and won't obey his orders. Foot stinging with the returning blood, he stumbles against
the man.

"I'm sorry," he repeats. "I thought it would be
OK to sleep there."

"*Anglais?*"

Danny nods.

"So where is your ticket?"

"I think I lost it."

"Then you come with me. We are in Barcelona. And you are in trouble!"

5

WHY THE KING WINKED

A vital hour is lost as Danny sits in an office at França Station and tries to work out an escape. The guard seems to take his stowing away personally. He doesn't for one minute buy Danny's story that he was traveling to meet a relative and had lost his ticket after getting on board.

"You are not on my list. So you are riding without a ticket. So I call the police."

Bad luck that he found me, Danny thinks. But then again, Dad used to say there was no such thing. "You make your own luck, good or bad, for yourself, old son." *So I was stupid. Perhaps there's a chance to make a dash for it, lose myself in the early morning rush hour.*

But other uniformed guards and policemen are visible through the glass door in the room beyond.

There's no window or other way out—and the man at the desk doesn't look like he's simply going to let his prisoner walk free. He's punching a number into the phone with a determined look on his face.

Frustrated, Danny fiddles with the new deck of playing cards from his pocket and starts to run them speedily through his fingers—cutting, shuffling, fanning. The man pauses and glances up: studying the boy, the rippling deck.

Danny catches that look and, sensing a chance, snaps the top card off the pack. King of hearts. He holds it up in a beam of sunlight, then flicks his hand, and the thing's gone. Such a quick sleight, so neatly done, that the mustachioed face of the king seems to wink—and then just vanish.

The guard raises his eyebrows. "You do tricks?"

Danny smiles. "*Oui.*"

"Why not show me one?"

"OK . . ." Danny says, sensing the turn of the tide, the hint of a smile around the corners of the man's eyes. "What would you like to see?"

"How about making that king appear again? He must be in your right hand still." He puts the handset back down gently on its cradle. "I do some magic myself . . ."

40

Got him!

"But then you should know that he isn't there," Danny says brightly. "He's already *long* gone. Look." He holds up his right hand, its back to the guard. Nothing there.

Then with a flick of the wrist, a curl of the fingers, he snaps his hand over to show an empty palm. "See? He's not there."

"*Alors*, where is he then?" the guard says, smiling broadly now, eager for the reveal, taking the bait.

"Right here, behind your ear!" Danny says, reaching forward, clipping the king smartly against the man's earlobe. The guard jumps, then beams, applauding silently.

"OK, *mon petit*. I'll make you a special deal. You show me that move for half an hour, teach me how to do it—and then I'll open the barriers for you and *phweeesssh*. Off you go. No questions asked. Ça va?"

"*Oui. Ça va*," Danny smiles.

The guard is true to his word. Forty minutes later, Danny is free and heading toward the Sagrada Familia in a taxi.

Barcelona is shaking itself awake to *café con leche* and deep-fried doughnuts, the roar of traffic, the pulse of commuters and early-rising tourists. Plane trees stand white in the autumn sunshine. There seems to be more graffiti than he remembers on the shutters of the shops and restaurants, more litter, more homeless people picking their way through the morning carrying bulging plastic bags. In Danny's memory Barcelona is bright, colorful, vital. Now it looks old and weary as it struggles to shake off the night. Harsher. Trick of the memory, perhaps?

Something else is definitely new: countless Catalonian flags hang from balconies, their red and yellow stripes twitching uneasily in the breeze.

How will it go, this reunion with the company? What's he going to say to Zamora, Rosa—to the Klowns? Anxiety tightens inside, a fist contracting in his stomach.

And how will *they* view him? Grief-stricken son of the cofounder of the troupe? A returning hero, fresh from real-life escapology in Hong Kong? Or an unwanted nuisance getting under their feet?

Worse than that, he thinks: *maybe the Forty-Nine will have its eyes trained on the venue. Maybe one of the company is out to get me. I could be going into the lion's den. Well, at least I'll have the element of surprise. Even if Laura's put out an alert, no one will know I'm here until I arrive . . . I've just got to act braver than I feel.*

The taxi swings around a corner, and there before him is the full glory of the Sagrada Familia thrusting itself up at the motionless clouds above. Any suspicion that his childish memory may have exaggerated the scale of the building is washed away. It's far bigger—crazier!—than he remembered. A mountain of stone and concrete, its towers and parapets encrusted with sculptures, dwarfing the neighboring buildings. Above all that, a crane is swinging its jib over the perpetual building site, the massive stone block suspended from it shrunk to nothing by the size of the towers.

What a venue! What a place for the Mysterium to spark back into life. There's even a long banner on the railings: in lettering as high as a person, that one magical word *MYSTERIUM*. It sets his pulse bounding.

It's real! I'm back, he thinks. At last the excitement is there too. It's hard to tell whether it's that or the nerves that make him fumble the change when the taxi driver takes the fee.

Danny clambers from the cab . . .

. . . and turns to find himself face to face with Darko Blanco.

The knife thrower's silver-gray eyes widen fractionally in surprise but hardly to the degree you'd expect. Then he raises his eyebrows—as if to acknowledge the peculiar way the world tends to work—and a smile breaks across his rugged, unshaven face.

"Danny. What brings you here?"

Darko's soft eastern European accent, so familiar, so easy, as if picking up the thread of a conversation interrupted by mere minutes, not a year and more. He's holding his black case in one hand, the one that carries his razor-sharp throwing knives. In the other he's balancing a cardboard tray of takeout coffees. A wild parakeet flashes green overhead, its call shredding the air.

"I heard about the reunion. I wanted to see it," Danny stumbles.

"Well, we're still a bit rusty. You'll have to be kind to us."

You don't seem very surprised to see me, Danny thinks, but then again, nothing much ever seemed to throw old Darko. The only time the man had seemed genuinely shaken was after the trailer fire when, ashen-faced, he had been withdrawn, silent, locked up in his own thoughts for days.

He stands gazing at Danny now, loose white shirt billowing, black boots planted firmly on the pavement. "You sure you're OK? You look a bit on edge."

Danny glances around at the crowds already streaming toward the Sagrada, eager to be off the street. "Can we go in?"

"Of course," Darko says. "Rosa's having a terrible day. Two days to showtime. And Zamora's all worked up about something."

"Are you all in there?" Danny asks, nodding at the vast body of the cathedral. "The Aerialisques? The Klowns . . . ?"

"All the regular crew," Darko says. "Except your dear old Mama and Papa, of course." He sighs and shakes his head. "And that rat Jimmy Torrini. Not expecting to see him again."

"I guess not," Danny says, moving quickly across the emotional thin ice. "But everyone else?"

"Yes, even Herzog is here," Darko says, as if following Danny's train of thought.

"How did you know I was thinking about Herzog?"

"Your eyes were scanning the pavement—for

someone short and friendly. Could only be Zamora or the dog. Looked less complicated than Zamora!"

Danny's forgotten how well Darko can do cold reading—almost as good as Dad used to do it. *Is he seeing straight through me now? He can tell I'm on edge. Perhaps I should tell him what I saw . . .*

But the knife thrower's already turned on his heels and leading the way past a line of tourists waiting for the cathedral to open.

Near the entrance, several shabbily dressed women are holding up cardboard signs and reaching out their hands toward anyone who comes near. Their faces are pinched and darkened by hunger. Grubby, dejected-looking children cling to their clothes. Hopeless.

"Can we give them something?" Danny asks.

"Doesn't really help," Darko Blanco says, "but I'm a soft touch. Here—check my right pocket."

One of the women is tugging at Darko's sleeve. From out of her bag she pulls two large oranges, offering them in exchange for the euros.

"*Gracias*," Darko says. "Here—take my case, Danny." That feels good. Taking the knife thrower's case gives him a role. A little toehold back in the company.

Perhaps I can help Frankie rig, he thinks. *Be useful.*

Holding the tray of coffee aloft on the finger-tips of his left hand, Darko takes the two oranges in his right and starts to juggle them in long, lazy arcs. Smiles break out on the children's faces.

"Come on, Danny. We can all get out of this with some dignity—if I don't drop the bleeding coffee . . ."

Twenty paces or so away, a figure in a green coat stands motionless in the line, her sunglasses reflecting the looping oranges, Darko, Danny, the cathedral's massive doorway. The sun splashes white on her short peroxide-blonde hair and half a smile on her face, but as to what is making her smile, it's impossible to say.

6

WHY THE LIGHT SMASHED

They enter the vast and luminous space of the cathedral.

Stained-glass light—purple, violet, pea green—filters down through the windows to reveal an interior that is part gothic cathedral, part sci-fi movie, like a temple for some alien religion. Balconies and spiral stairways cling to the walls, while a forest of stone columns floats thousands of tons of biscuit-colored stone up and over their heads. The air is still and cool.

Expectation and worry are quickstepping Danny's pulse again. "Whatever you do, old son," Dad used to say, "when you grow up, promise me that you'll dare to be a Daniel. When you have to enter the lion's den, do it with your head held high . . ."

So Danny raises his chin, lengthens his stride, trying to look confident and match Darko's casual ease. As if he belongs.

At the far end a large chunk of the nave has been blocked off behind temporary screening.

"We're down here," the knife thrower says, still effortlessly cycling the oranges. Not a drop of coffee spilled. "Best venue ever."

But Danny isn't really listening to his voice—his ears are straining for something else.

And then he hears it. The sound of his childhood: the metallic jangle and clink of rigging—wire and rope and carabiner rapping against scaffolding, voices calling from above, serious, measured.

He hurries after Darko, through a gap in the screen, and steps back into the world of a circus company preparing for action. Before they see him, he sees them, all brightly lit in the sting of the arc lights.

Two of the Aerialisques—identical Izzy and Beatrice—hang upside down on their scarlet silks, hair tumbling toward the stone floor far below. Just above them is Frankie B., leaning nonchalantly from the scaffolding rig, one strong arm working away with a wrench, the cluster of carabiners and slings ringing away at his belt. On the ground, Maria, the

Australian aerialist, is looking up, mouth open in concern, strong tattooed arms anchoring the dangling silk, while Bjorn, heavyset, prowls in the background, rubbing chalk on his hands, puffing white clouds of the stuff around his strong head. Aki and Joey are doing stretching exercises together back-to-back, biceps flexing powerfully. Nearby, Billy crouches over his effects pedals with a puzzled look on his face, one hand stroking his thick beard.

And there behind them is Rosa, hands on hips, staring at Zamora as if trying to read his thoughts. The dwarf himself is rooted to the ground, a mobile phone pressed to one ear, stubby index finger rammed in the other.

Over everything hangs the aroma of chalk and rosin and sweat and warm lights. It's all so powerful, so familiar. The sounds of the past, the smells of the past. No one and nothing has changed in the last eighteen months. *Only me*, Danny thinks.

It seems incredible that Mum and Dad will not suddenly step out from the wings—Dad clapping his hands and calling the rehearsal to order and Mum going quietly, half a smile on her face, to her position at the bottom of a ladder, to wait for her cue. But it's not going to happen, is it?

"As if by magic," Darko says over his shoulder. "The Mysterium reborn."

That fist is tightening in Danny's stomach now. Yes—there's a smile lifting his face, but at the same time he has the feeling he might be sick. *Hold onto it*, he thinks. *I never thought I would be here again, never thought I'd hear these sounds, see these people—*

A jarring burst of feedback rips through the sound system, and the spell is broken. Billy holds up his hand in apology. "Sorry!" he calls. "Wrong pedal." Everyone looks up, but it is Herzog who sees Danny first. Barking, claws skittering on the polished stone floor, he comes bounding across the performance space, ears flapping, knocking against Maria.

"Stupid dog! Calm him down, Darko."

She turns to see where Herzog is going, then lets out a cry. "My God," she shouts, "it's Danny!"

Herzog thumps his paws onto Danny's chest, tongue seeking out his face. Beatrice and Izzy give twin cries of delight and come tumbling down the silks, while Rosa turns, her mouth framing a perfect round "O" of surprise. Zamora's eyes widen, his attention snapped from the phone, the index finger now pointing at Danny.

And then the members of the company are

surrounding him, showering him with greetings, ruffling his hair.

"Gosh, you've grown!"

"How *are* you?"

"What are you doing here?!"

Rosa comes pushing through the throng. "Danny! *Bello!* So good to see you. But you've been a bad boy, I think . . ."

Danny's trying to answer everyone, but at the same time keep half an eye on their reactions, particularly the Klowns.

Everyone seems genuinely pleased to see him, though. Even Aki has managed a smile, and Bjorn is shaking his head in disbelief, muttering away under his breath. Joey is running his hand through his bright red hair and nodding, as if in agreement with himself. *Must keep my wits about me*, Danny thinks. *Must keep my eyes open for any little clue.* But there's just too much to take in all at once.

And then Zamora is there.

Unlike the others, the Major isn't smiling. His face is stiffened by anger, as if facing a strong wind.

"Mister Danny! What on God's green earth do you think you're doing? Laura's worried sick. At least now I can tell her you haven't got lost or been run down by a car—"

"Major, I—"

"Not a word! It was wrong to run away from her, Danny. Quite wrong!"

"But I didn't run *away*. I was running *to* something. To see you!"

"That's not the point," Zamora snaps. He glares around at the others. "*Carajo!* Give us some space, won't you? I'm his godfather, so it's my business. Everyone's got work to do, so get on with it!"

The others back away, eyebrows raised. Despite Zamora's anger, Danny has enough awareness to spot how quickly the smile extinguishes itself from Joey's face, as if wiped clean. And how Aki catches the Frenchman's eye then and gives a quick shake of the head. Something conspiratorial in that glance? Maybe a warning.

"Are you listening to me, Mister Danny?" Zamora growls, planting a firm hand on Danny's arm. "Your parents made plans for Laura to be your guardian—not me—for a reason! Understand?"

"And why did they do that in advance?" Danny snaps back. So much has happened behind his back— so much secrecy and evasion—and he's had enough of it. "*Why?!*"

Zamora spreads his arms wide, flailing for the right words. "Because, Danny, they . . . knew they did dangerous jobs, because—"

"And why didn't *you* tell me the Mysterium was re-forming?"

The Major looks away, pushing his tongue against the wall of his cheek, regaining his composure. The question hangs in the air between them.

"Why, Major?"

"I'm sorry, *amigo*. Very sorry. I just thought maybe it would be too painful for you—too soon. And we've all got lives to be getting on with, you know, bills to pay. It's not just about you . . ."

Danny looks away now, the words hitting home, smarting.

"No. That's not what I meant to say," the Major stumbles. "Look. I'm sorry to get cross, but I was worried too! Ever since Laura phoned me at three this morning! And I've been up ever since. I must call her back at once."

"We need to talk," Danny whispers. "It's urgent. There might be trouble here—"

"Two shakes, Danny. Let me calm your blooming aunt down first. Give me a moment to get my own temper down, no?"

The others are still casting interested but concerned looks in Danny's direction. Rosa is standing a few paces away, pushing a hand through her tumble of auburn hair.

"Tell you what, *bello*," she says, "you come with me for a few minutes and let the Major sort things out. You hungry?"

"I need to talk to Zamora."

"Go with Rosa," Zamora snaps—and then softens his face, an apologetic smile. "Then we'll talk."

So far, apart from that quick look that passed between Joey and Aki, there's been nothing suspicious in the reactions of the company. The worst of Danny's nerves are calming a bit, even if there's still a tangle of emotion writhing around in the pit of his stomach.

The ringmistress leads him across the performance space, over the familiar sprawl of coiled rigging rope, anchor points, wires, chalked crosses marking key performance spots. She glances over her shoulder. "And you got here all by yourself, *bello*? That's imp—"

"Heads!" Frankie's voice, bellowing from above, cuts her short.

A fraction later, there's an explosion. A spotlight, loosened from the track above, has dropped to the floor, crashing, splintering apart on the flagstones. Chips of reflective glass and bulb are sent flying through the air, and a bright fragment fizzes past Danny's nose. The sound reverberates like a bomb in the immensity of the Sagrada's interior, echoing back off the columns and walls. Instinctively, Danny has braced himself, waiting for worse, his body on alert, remembering the explosion at school. But that's it. Silence returns.

Rosa glowers up at Frankie. He's about ten paces farther along the scaffolding, looking down, his mouth hanging open in alarm.

"What was that, Frankie!?"

"Jeez. Dunno how that happened. I locked that one up." He extends a hand in apology, but Rosa shakes her head, stomping across the wreckage in her calf-length boots, crunching the glass underfoot.

"*Idiota!* Could have brained me. Or the boy." Danny's sharp eyes flicker from the broken spotlight to Frankie Boom and back again.

That was close, he thinks. *Just a few more paces and*

it would've hit me. At that height, at that speed . . . it doesn't bear thinking about. Maybe it was just an accident. Maybe.

Frankie gazes down at him, the light reflected off his smooth bald head.

"Sorry, kid. Dangerous place, the circus, sometimes . . ." He waves another apology and shifts farther along the track.

Maybe I am in the lion's den, Danny thinks.

"And remember this," Dad also used to say. "When you're in it, you might just need to punch that stupid lion right on the nose."

The first tourists have been admitted to the cathedral, and drawn by the sound of the falling spotlight, one or two are peeking through a gap in the screen.

One woman pauses to take a photo.

The boy is still looking up into the rigging. She lines him up carefully in the crosshairs before pressing the shutter, then stashes the camera away in the pocket of her green coat, before slipping away into the crowd.

7

WHY DAD HAD AN OPINION ABOUT EVERYTHING

The accident with the spotlight has done little to calm Danny's wired nerves.

As Rosa leads him to where a handful of the Mysterium's vehicles are huddled in the cathedral's shadow, Danny glances up again at the dizzying towers, the yellow cranes slow-motioning across the sky, that massive block of stone still poised over their heads.

"Hope that didn't make you jump too much, *bello*?"

"No. I'm fine," he lies. He wants to act tough, to *be* tough, to show Rosa that he's circus through and through. But inside it's another matter.

"Good," Rosa says. "There was just room

enough for my little caravan back here. I don't like hotels, and the director should be on hand. Cracking the whip!"

Danny manages a smile, glad that his first real interaction with the company will be with Rosa.

Despite her feisty manner and the parts of her act that made him uncomfortable (fish, knitting needles), he always felt she looked on him as a family member. Again, that memory comes to him now as he follows her to the caravan: the night she found him hidden away in the prop store and led him across the snow-choked encampment, Dad's Escape Book tucked under his arm. The *ribollita* stew simmering on her caravan stove, filling the air with its reassuring aroma. And then the alarm was raised, and they raced too late to the inferno of the family trailer, and then—

"I was doing my tarot cards," she says brightly, opening the caravan door. "Kept coming up with an unexpected visitor. And now here you are! I'm never wrong, *bello*."

Danny slides onto the bench seat. "Rosa," he says, trying to choose his words carefully, "what happened—after Berlin? I mean, how come you're all back together?"

"Didn't Zamora tell you?"

"Not really." It hurts to say it out loud, to admit that the Major didn't include him in the plans.

Rosa shrugs. "No great mystery. Everyone was so shocked, so upset about your Mama and Papa. We didn't want to do them dishonor by carrying on, so we dissolved the company and went and did our own things. Darko's gone into business in Berlin. Doing really well, apparently. The girls were with Circa for a bit. Joey and Bjorn were in CirkVost, and Billy was in Brooklyn with Aki . . . But what's this about Hong Kong!? You and Zamora and a ladder? Sounds crazy!"

"It's a long story," Danny says. Odd that Rosa hasn't jumped straight to the underwater escape. Does she not know, then?

The ringmistress motions him to sit down. She strikes a match and lights the gas ring, setting the kettle on its blue flame, and then chucks the matchbox onto the table in front of Danny. It bounces and lands label side up, matches rattling, exposing a fierce-looking tiger. The bold striped design catches Danny's eye.

"That's one of Javier's clubs," Rosa says brightly. "The Tigressa, up on the hill. Nice, huh?"

"Javier?"

"Surely you remember him? Big man. Zamora and him used to be like brothers."

Danny shakes his head.

"That's memory for you. But you were very small when you last saw him. He's our booking agent here."

Danny shakes his head. *Can't remember,* he thinks. *And it doesn't matter now!* "Tell me how you all got back together."

"Well, after a year had gone past, Darko and Zamora started e-mailing. And then they dragged me away from my show. They felt we were too good an outfit not to perform again. *I* said they should let you know, but Zamora felt we should wait—"

"I *wish* he'd told me."

"Ah," Rosa says, "if wishes were fishes, we'd all have a lot of fish, right?"

"Jimmy T. used to say that."

A shadow darkens Rosa's face. "Poor old Jimmy. One member of the company we don't need back, though, I guess. Your Papa did the right thing."

Right thing about what? Surely Jimmy just packed up and left. Danny feels his jaw tightening, as he holds back the question. *Can't chase every thought*, he thinks, *got to stick with the things I need to know right now—the vital elements.*

"Can I ask you something else?"

"Try me."

"The night Mum and Dad died, did you see anything—"

"No!" Rosa shakes her head vigorously. But she isn't answering the question, she's shaking away the subject. "No, Danny. You have to let it go. You *have* to. Otherwise, the sadness will just eat you up. *I* know that!"

"But Mum and Dad were so careful."

"We all make mistakes. And then there's just sheer bad luck. In circus and in life just the same. Doesn't matter who you are."

"Dad always said you make your own luck."

"Your Dad had a bleeding opinion about everything, Danny. Excuse me. But sometimes things just happen. Period."

"That's what Aunt Laura says," Danny mumbles, feeling defensive for Dad but knowing Rosa has a point.

And he can see that her mood has changed abruptly. She saws through some bread, slaps chunks of chorizo sausage and cheese between, and then cuts the sandwich in half with the big bread knife, irritation snagging her movements.

"I just wanted—"

"Eat!" she says, putting the sandwich down on the table in front of him. "Let the other stuff go, Danny. For your sake—and for the rest of us too. I'm glad to see you, but don't go stirring up the past. Let it rest in peace. It's better for everyone."

Better for everyone but me, Danny thinks. But he takes a bite of the sandwich, to be polite, to keep Rosa on his side. And because, suddenly, he's realized just how hungry he is.

There's a knock on the door, and Zamora pops his head through. His face looks calmer, and he smiles at the sight of Danny attempting to devour the thick sandwich.

"I've just done you an *enormous* favor, Mister Danny. Think I've saved your life. Laura wanted to strangle you."

Danny stops mid bite, anxious again. What's the decision, then? "Don't make me go back . . ." he mumbles through a full mouth.

But Zamora holds up his hands, a calming, quieting gesture. "Not only have I soothed her savage brow, *amigo*, I've even got her to agree to let you stay until the first performance. Then she's coming to get you. No arguing then. She thinks it should be safe enough."

Yes! He sighs inwardly. That's as good as he's hoped for—better!

"Safe?" Rosa says sharply. "What d'you mean?"

"With us no-good circus types," Zamora adds hastily.

Danny nods, taking another bite at the sandwich.

"Thought you'd be overjoyed," Zamora says, flapping his arms in mild frustration.

"I am." He swallows hard. "But I need to talk to you. Now."

Rosa whisks the singing kettle from the gas ring. "You can have the morning off if you want, Zamora. It's all tech-run. But we need to do a full rehearsal this afternoon. Including your cannon."

"OK," the Major says to Danny. "We'll head to an old haunt of mine in the Gothic Quarter. And talk. We could go to that magic shop you liked. And then later, you will have the privilege of seeing one of my last ever flights as a human cannonball!"

As they go back through the performance space, Frankie comes hopping down the rope ladder. For a big man he lands surprisingly lightly on his sneakered feet.

"Just gonna clear up," he says, flashing a quick smile at Danny. "Hope it didn't make ya jump, kiddo."

"No," Danny lies, watching Frankie carefully.

The rigger bends down and, from amongst the wreckage, plucks a shiny metal loop—a carabiner. He looks at it for a moment, puzzled, then screws the fastening nut tight and tugs at it.

"Weird," he says, and then tosses the metal ring to Danny. "New one. But I can't risk using it, not after a bash like that. You always liked to play with 'em. When you was a little kid."

"Thanks," Danny says. He's about to repeat that he's not a little kid anymore but then decides he wants to keep as many people sympathetic as possible. Any member of the company might hold the clue or memory fragment that will help solve the puzzle. He pockets the carabiner, scrutinizing Frankie's face.

The bald man returns his gaze. "Hey, don't give me the eyes, man!" he laughs. "Used to freak me out when your Dad did that!"

Another storm of feedback howls from Billy's amp as his guitar starts to throb through the great cathedral. It sounds ominous, mysterious, insistent. Once that mixture would have filled Danny with pleasure—but now it just stokes his sense of foreboding.

8

WHY ZAMORA DIDN'T GET HIS DRINK

A short metro ride takes them back downtown. Danny's glad to be on his own with his friend at last—but still that sense of betrayal is clouding his thoughts. How could the Major have kept so silent about something so huge? The rebirth of the Mysterium! *Got to try and forget about it*, he thinks. *Can't let it mess up our friendship.*

For his part, Zamora keeps up a barrage of questions about the nighttime flight from Paris. It's almost as if he's trying to stall Danny from talking and seems, from time to time, to be glancing over his shoulder at their fellow passengers. When the Major pauses for breath, Danny takes his chance.

"I need to tell you about something I saw on Laura's iPad—"

Zamora holds his finger to his lips, casting an eye at the packed carriage. "Hold it a *momentito*, Mister Danny. I've a feeling I'm going to need a strong *café solo* for this. Or maybe a beer."

"OK," Danny says, trying to keep calm, keen to unburden himself of the image of the dead man, the dots.

They emerge from the metro and cross the wide-open space of Plaça de Catalunya. Fountains dance in the breeze, and Danny feels their cold spray ghost across his face. Despite the sunshine, you can feel colder weather is on the way, a chill in the shadows.

The Major grimaces. "That old break in my leg's aching. Always means there's stormy weather coming. Or bad luck!"

"So you think there might be trouble here too?"

The Major squints into the sun. "Something's not right. Just don't know what. Hold onto your bag—still a lot of pickpockets 'round here."

They cross the surging traffic and plunge into the heady swirl of Las Ramblas. Tourists hold up camcorders and mobiles to record the scene, to capture the living statues with their skins spray-painted gold or silver, the tango dancers, flamenco buskers— all squashed between stalls selling flowers of every color, squawking birds in cages. For once it isn't the sight of Zamora that draws people's eyes.

A bronze-winged demon sculpture suddenly roars into life, flaps his wings, and grabs hold of a startled teenage girl, who screams . . . and everyone else laughs. Danny and Zamora are caught in the jostle as the crowd reacts, recoiling from the demon— and a woman in a green coat bumps against him.

"Oh! *Lo siento!*" she calls out in apology before being promptly swallowed by the crowd.

Nearby, a huddle of illegal traders, with bracelets and bird whistles spread on blankets, are touting for business. They flick bright smiles at the passing crowd—but anxiety shades their eyes as they watch for the police.

Zamora has thrust his hands in his pockets.

"Bit too touristy, no? My Barcelona is the backstreets. El Raval, Gothic Quarter—"

Danny holds up a hand. Normally Zamora's memories of his youth would be something to revel in . . . but not now! "Major! It's about the Forty-Nine. I think they're here. In Barcelona."

Zamora stops dead in the middle of the hustle of Las Ramblas. "No way. You can't be serious."

"I'm sure. That's why I came."

But now that he says it out loud, it sounds unlikely—fantastical even. *Perhaps my imagination's working overtime*, Danny thinks. "I was worried, so I came to Barcelona. To make sure you were OK."

Somewhere in the distance there's a siren swaying on the breeze and the illegal traders are looking nervous, undecided about whether to pack up their wares or chance a few more minutes. And from farther down Las Ramblas, away to the left, there's a kind of rhythmic chanting starting up, voices raised in unison, just audible over the hum of the crowd.

Zamora cocks his head. "But the Forty-Nine? Come off it. Ricard said there's no evidence they're real."

"I saw a photo. There was a body up at the fairground. Tibi-something. And someone had *burned* the dotted pattern onto his back."

The Major pulls a face, doubt—but now also anxiety—stamped across his features. —"Tibidabo? You're sure?"

"That's what the article said."

"Maybe we need to take a bit more care, then," Zamora grunts. "Maybe get you out of here—"

"I'm staying."

"You might try listening to me, Mister Danny. Main thing is to keep you safe."

"The main thing is to find out what's going on!" Danny fires back.

"I don't know. Laura wants you back ASAP. But I can ask around. Javier has . . . um . . . connections that might help." Zamora puffs out his cheeks. "I guess it can't be a coincidence, can it?"

Danny shakes his head, relieved that Zamora isn't dismissing him out of hand. But at the same time it makes the whole thing seem more real. Scarier.

The chanting is getting louder, a tune picking itself out in the massed voices, and Zamora raises himself onto his tiptoes to see what's happening. "Sounds like a demonstration. Can you see, Danny? Could be an independence rally . . ."

He's cut short by the siren that suddenly whoops right behind them now. Shouts of alarm spike through the crowd, and Danny spins around to work out what is happening. One of the merchants gives a whistle, and the traders yank their blankets together by the strings tied to their corners. They take off through the crowd, bundles bouncing heavily on their shoulders, fear burning their eyes.

"*Carajo*. Riot police," Zamora groans. "Just what we need."

A phalanx of black-helmeted police are forcing their way through the alarmed tourists and stallholders. They're going full charge, their sticks raised, ready to deliver a blow to anyone who seems to be making trouble. A Chinese tourist steps in front, trying to film them on his tablet, and the next second he's *flying*, the expensive screen shattering on the pavement. Danny goes to help the man, but Zamora tugs him back.

"Take cover," he says. "Some of these boys are just plain loco."

The police thunder past. Their eyes, just visible over scarves masking the rest of their faces, are intent on the fleeing traders. Danny watches, edging back from the middle of the street, feeling uneasy at the display of aggression, his own eyes following the traders, quietly rooting for them—but something's prickling now at the back of his skull: a nagging animal instinct—a sixth sense—warning of imminent personal danger behind.

He looks around.

Three riot police are trailing the others, moving more slowly, heads turning this way and that like prowling wolves, scanning the crowd. Then one of them looks straight at Danny. He turns to shout something at his two colleagues—and all three accelerate toward *him*. Fear and shock jolt through Danny's body, threatening to fix him to the spot.

Zamora sees them too. He pushes Danny away down the street with both hands, urging him to action. "Run, Danny! For God's sake."

Zamora turns to block the policemen—but he's caught off-balance, and the first of them bangs into him hard with his shoulder, sending the Major sprawling.

Danny's survival instincts take over. He pushes away through the crowd, the three riot police just a handful of paces behind him, closing fast. Through the tinted visors, his pursuers' eyes glitter unpleasant intent. They're almost within reach. But then Danny's speed, his agility, take over. Quickly he widens the gap as he weaves between shoppers and tourists, down Las Ramblas toward the harbor and the sea beyond.

He glances back. What's happened to Zamora? Impossible to see, and the black helmets are only ten paces or so behind, bobbing through the crowd. No time to wait.

What do the police want with him? It can't be about the fare dodging back on the train! Surely they're after the merchants—or maybe the demonstration or whatever it is ahead. *Maybe they're not after me at all?*

But one quick glance over his shoulder tells him that they are. Still coming straight for him, barging people out of the way with their riot shields, the dull thud of the impacts silencing shouts of protest from the few student-y types who try to block their way.

What and *why* can wait. The familiar surge of adrenaline is short-circuiting rational thought. *Run, Danny.*

The crowds on Las Ramblas are packed tight, but while they're good for camouflage, they make it hard to get up much speed. Danny dances from foot to foot, doing his best to dodge around the confused, panicky tourists. Looking for space, he brushes the corner of a flower stall and slams into the back of a fat man who inadvertently blocks his way at the last minute. This is stupid—time to take to the backstreets.

He hurdles over a bench and cuts left down a narrow passageway, out of the bright sun and into a deep shadow, his footsteps loud on the cobbles. Far fewer pedestrians here, so he can cross the ground quickly, but now he's broken cover—and in full view. Glancing over his shoulder he sees the two black-clad figures silhouetted against the street beyond. They pause briefly—and then come pounding down the dark, narrow alleyway. The fear drags hard at his stomach.

Danny remembers enough of Barcelona to know that this side of Las Ramblas is a warren of old, tight streets. The Gothic Quarter. Easy to get lost in—but easy to lose people too. He's got about ten seconds' head start, so there may be enough time to disappear into the labyrinth with a few quick turns.

The street he's on feels vaguely familiar. He corners hard to the right, but—in his scramble to get out of sight—his foot catches the curb and he stumbles badly.

His arms spread to try and keep his balance, but it's no good, he's going too fast, and his body braces for impact on the pavement. But the blow doesn't come.

Maybe it's the circus gods reaching out to help.

Or, maybe, Danny's feet have taken him in a half-remembered direction, toward friendly ground. Maybe it's just luck . . .

But two very strong hands catch his forearms, arresting his fall, swinging him back up like a caught flyer on the trapeze. Deep laughter fills his ears, drowning for a moment the fear punching through his system. Strangely hollow.

"*Bon dia!*"

Danny looks up—and straight into the eyes of a devil.

He can only think for a moment that he's banged his skull and is suffering some kind of concussion. Leering down at him is an enormous red face, its eyes wide and staring, the mouth brightly painted, the expression on the whole thing stiff, unreal, nightmarish.

"Can I help you?" the voice booms from somewhere inside the hollow head. It must be three feet wide—looming over him.

Danny glances around, and the penny drops. He's outside the shop front of El Ingenio—the magic and theatrical shop—its window packed with carnival masks, fright wigs, painted *capgros* festival heads, magic tricks. A favorite memory of his earlier visits—a place where his tightly guarded pocket money would be spent within five minutes. But the circumstances are so different now.

The policemen's boots are thumping down the street toward them, and Danny struggles to free himself from the devil's embrace. The papier-mâché head laughs again, the whole thing shaking as if convulsed by a fit. "*No parla Catala*—?"

"Help me. Please!"

The devil picks out the desperation in Danny's voice and opens his arms, releasing him at once. Turning his monstrous head, he sees the riot police. He growls a curse through the slit of the reddened mouth and moves to face the men, blocking the alleyway as they charge.

"Go on, kid. Run!"

The police are on him. He manages to body-check one of the men, shoving him up hard against the stone wall, but the second gives him a violent blow to the small of the back that makes him stagger and then brings his stick down full force on the crown of that enormous bloodred head, cracking the thing clean in two.

It's a shocking, surreal image that stops the policemen in their tracks for a few vital seconds and gives Danny his chance. He accelerates away, through the deep blue shadows of the passageway, his stride lengthening, buoyed by the intervention of the giant, but aware that the police are still not far behind.

The streets are tiny here, closed to traffic. The metal shutters, still down on many shops and cafés, amplify the sound of the chasing boots. Danny cuts across a staggered intersection, down another narrow passage, and suddenly out into brilliant sunshine again.

He's in a plaza bathed in light, with elegant yellow buildings on all sides and palm trees erupting from the flagstones on dead straight trunks. Their leaves are long dark slashes in the sky overhead.

Which way? Which way now?

The place is almost empty, just a few people sipping morning coffee. A couple of tramps picking through a garbage can—and two regular uniformed policemen on the far side.

From behind come the shouts of the riot police. *Can't risk explaining myself to the uniformed men,* Danny thinks, *and I can't go right—that's back to Las Ramblas and the rest of them.* In the stillness of the square he hears again that growing, rhythmic chanting. The same tune but picking up speed—as if building toward a crescendo. Away to the left but closer now.

Why not? *Might be able to lose myself in whatever's happening there.*

The uniformed regular officers are taking an interest now, strolling across between the palm trees toward Danny. One of them is bringing a whistle to his lips. Seeing Danny turn on his heels, the second one starts to jog.

"*Para! Policia!*"

But they're too slow.

He's away again, down another tunnel of a street. No time for strategy now, it's just a question of fight or flight—and fighting doesn't seem like a good option.

At least his body feels strong again, with reserves yet to be tapped in his legs and heart. All those days training alongside the Khaos Klowns and Aerialisques, going through stretching routines and building stamina and strength, alive again in his body now. At Ballstone—on all the afternoons standing miserably on the mud-gripped football fields—it lay dormant. Now it flows through him: strong legs, poise, balance. Feels good, feels right.

There's another brightly lit square opening ahead and a surge of people heading toward it. Most of them are dressed the same way, with baggy white shirts bound by red sashes. The singing is louder now, booming down the alleyway, and a drum has picked up a steady beat, powering the song along, supported by thin-voiced instruments. A few tourists are hurrying the same way, video cameras and phones in hand. Something worth seeing, then, presumably? Not just a political demonstration.

He bursts into the square—and into a dead end. The whole of the space is crammed with people, pressed up against one another in a solid, tight mass of bodies. The music is suddenly very loud, picking up speed and intensity, and the crowd sings as one. No way through, Danny realizes, and—for the first time—panic threatens to lock him up.

He looks around, hoping that maybe he has lost his pursuers—but no such luck. Dark forms are visible in the shadows. The helmeted men are still coming.

Seeing that their quarry is cornered, they have dropped their speed to a brisk walk, pushing past the onlookers, closing in with each stride, batons in hand.

9

WHY DANNY HAD TO JUMP

Danny turns back to scan the square, his body taut, breath ragged. *Must be a way out of this, though*, he thinks.

The scrum of bodies is impenetrable, all facing the same way, curving around a fixed point in the far corner, all eyes raised, riveted on whatever is happening above that. It's only now that Danny looks up and sees the focus of that attention.

Raising itself from the heaving crowd of bodies is a human tower. Some six layers high, its foundation is a ring of twenty or so men standing on the shoulders of the supporting base. Then, tapering up into the sunshine: five men stand bound on the next level, with four on the one above that, and then three lighter, smaller figures—teenagers, maybe.

And another layer climbing into place after that, into the sunshine. The singing is full power now, hypnotic, the crowd pushing at the base of the tower to lend it their strength. At the top, three children are interlocking arms and steadying themselves on the dizzying height, swaying just an arm's length or so from a fourth-floor balcony.

The final tier already climbing up toward the top . . .

Danny looks back. Behind him one of the riot police is laying into a young man who has dared to warn them off. It's an ugly glimpse of what awaits him if he's caught, their batons flashing as they strike.

His mouth is dry now—but an idea is taking hold of him, and once it's whispered its thought, there's nothing he can do but follow it. So mad, so glorious—a performer's escape route. It's not unlike going up the rigging into the hemisphere, after all. And he's been on a three-up pyramid before—admittedly with a safety wire, but he was never going to fall, not even when Joey deliberately made him wobble.

Danny grabs hold of the sash of the man in front, plants his foot, and pulls himself up onto his shoulders. Then, quickly, with groans and shouts of complaint from under his shoes, he picks his way across the tightly packed cluster of the tower's support base. The music picks up speed again, lifting the crowd to new efforts, raising Danny's own spirits, making him believe that the impossible might just be possible. After all, every act needs its music.

Perhaps there is no need to go farther? Perhaps he can just cross this sea of bodies and drop down into the street beyond. He looks ahead, peering past the pyramid, but sees more police in the alley. Only one way to go, then. And somewhere at the back of his mind, he is glad. He wants to try the thing now, the mix of fear and excitement sending him forward across this walkway of shoulders and arms and backs. *Try and stop me*, he thinks—and he's at the foot of the tower proper.

Someone's shouting at him, but he's already climbing, doing it just the way he saw the last three climbers mount, using handholds on the sashes, feet on hips. The structure sways as he clambers past the second level. Then he steadies himself and climbs on up the back of a strongly built man who's muttering encouragement to the sweating, straining people making up the third tier. One of them sees Danny. He looks puzzled and starts to say something, but then—perhaps held by those intense green and brown eyes, the desperate look shining from them—closes his mouth again and nods in shared determination.

Danny glances down. It already seems high, but the massed bodies below are reassuring. A human safety net. Another foothold on a thick red sash, another hand on a shoulder, another head passes beneath him. On the other side of the tower, a small boy in a gleaming red crash helmet is climbing steadily but surely, a flag gripped between his teeth, the summit climber of the human mountain—but Danny is going faster. He overtakes the astonished boy, feeling guilt for stealing the boy's thunder, for racing to the top first. But there's no going back now and his need is greater. Nearly there . . .

But the tower shakes then, sagging toward the buildings. Danny loses his foothold, hanging precariously over the drop, both hands gripping the belt of a wiry teenager on the penultimate layer. There's a groan from the entire edifice as everyone applies their strength to rebalance, a gasp from the crowd. And then he has his footing again, is up onto the back of the last level.

He twists to scope out the fourth-floor balcony. It's packed with young people, filming, cheering, laughing—so close. Danny allows himself one quick look down, then motions to the people on the balcony to get out of the way—and launches himself sideways with all his strength, hoping in that fleeting moment that he's done enough, judged it right. He's always heard the expression "heart in mouth." Now he knows what that feels like.

His shin bangs the balcony railing, and he tumbles into the students in a muddle of legs and arms. From below comes a massive cheer—but it's not for him alone. As he's helped to his feet, Danny sees the young boy standing triumphantly at the top of the tower, waving a Catalan flag. Then he's shimmying down and the whole edifice is crumbling, dismantling itself as fast as possible. Danny scans the chaotic crowd below. No sign of the black helmets. Where are they?

American voices are filling his ears.

"Hey man, that was so cool," one girl says, patting him on the back. "Why don't you have a costume too?"

"I'm not really part of it," Danny stutters, his eyes still fixed on the square below. Maybe they've anticipated his move. Maybe they're already heading for this building . . .

"Man, that's the best *castell* we've seen this

summer," another of the students is saying. "Eight layers—never seen anyone jump from the top."

Danny nods and then pushes his way past the admiring faces, darting into the living room, desperately hunting for the front door.

I've got to move fast, he thinks. *They'll know which building I'm in. Probably only got a minute or so.*

He finds himself in an elegant stairwell. An elevator shaft drops into the shadows below. *If the police are already at the door, I'll be trapped*, he thinks, *but they won't expect me to keep going up. That worked in Hong Kong. And the gaps between the buildings are so tight I won't even need a ladder! I've seen Joey do it often enough . . .*

He hurtles up the wooden stairs two at a time, ears straining for the sound of feet in the stairwell. Still nothing but the quick step of his own trainers. In this brief lull his thoughts turn to Zamora. What has happened to the Major? Already being roughed up in some riot van? Unconscious and bleeding on the pavement? *I just hope he's OK*, Danny thinks. *I can't cope without him.*

The elevator machinery is whirring—a wood-framed glass box dropping past him, looking for all the world like something from an escapology routine. Someone must have called it.

Get a flipping move on, Sing Sing would say. He wishes for a moment that she was there beside him—not just for her kung fu moves but for the strength in her eyes, her stubborn survivor's pride. *I'll tell her about this*, he thinks. *One day I'll tell her, and she'll laugh about it in that way of hers.* The thought puts new energy into his legs.

The grand stairway ends abruptly on a wide landing. Beyond that, a smaller flight of steps leads to a door onto a roof terrace. Through the glass panel he can see a jumble of crumbling flowerpots, TV antennae, clothes drying on a line, cheap plastic furniture stained by the rain.

Locked.

The elevator is coming back up now, and the heavy tread of boots drumming the steps tells him there's not much time.

Fingers shaking, he takes Dad's lock pick set from around his neck, selects the S-rake, and drags it in and out of the simple mechanism, turning the door handle at the same time and pushing. Shouldn't even need the tensioning tool on something like this. *Come on. Come on!* The footsteps are just a couple of floors below. Why won't the stupid lock go? All the pins are back, he can't feel them resisting, so it should open—

He gives the door a final shove and then steps back, ready to kick the handle as hard as he can . . .

. . . and the door gently swings open, toward him. *Probably wasn't even actually locked*, he thinks as he darts through it. That's what happens when you're going too fast. You miss the obvious.

He picks his way across the roof, dodging under the dancing laundry, to a low railing. Another terrace just a few paces away, and beyond that a rising and falling roofscape of tiles, terraces, chimneys, balconies—all sliced through with dark crevasses where the alleys of the Gothic Quarter run. No time for anything fancy. No time to assess all the risks. *They're almost on me. Just free run and improvise.*

He takes four paces back and runs hard, planting his foot on the rusty handrail, pushing with all his might through that leg, transferring speed into lift. And then he's hanging in the air for a second, the wind rushing his ears, and then landing, *oooof,* his knees and ankles jarring, buckling, on the slightly lower roof beyond. He regains his balance and glances back.

Sunlight reflects off the black helmets as the men dash toward the railing, voices thick with malice but now frustration.

"*Para!*"

Danny doesn't wait. He sprints up a tiled roof as if he's about to take off into the blue sky, throws himself recklessly over the crest, and goes scrambling and sliding down the other side. He lands in a heap, rolls, and without pausing powers across another roof terrace, before hurdling over another gap above a tiny slit of a street. This time, he sees the drop beneath him, the tiny figures in the alleyway, and wishes he hadn't.

A fire escape to his right. Danny puts his hands on the smooth rail, lifts his feet in the air, and drops the length of it, landing with a clang on a metal balcony. An easy jump from that to a lower roof. Then quickly, arms out, across the top of an archway that curves over a broader street, onto an inclined buttress that shores up a medieval house, all tiny bricks and precarious angles that lead to a turret.

In the rush of the skills, the pure exhilaration of tackling each obstacle, he has almost forgotten his pursuers! That should be enough now, though—no way would they have followed him through all that.

He shimmies through an open window and finds himself on a spiral staircase—and then he races down and down, three full floors, until he is spun out into a shadowed courtyard. A long line of people are waiting patiently for admission to the museum behind him, and some of them turn to look curiously at the young boy breathing hard, steadying himself against the wall.

Danny's heart is pounding with the effort of his aerial escape. How many minutes did his flight take? No more than ten. Now, struggling to get his breath back, the effort, the fear of the chase, the danger of his climb up the human tower all come surging at him. Rosa's sandwich churning in his stomach. Legs shaking.

He realizes he's about to be sick.

A sign for toilets. An arrow. He just about makes it into a cubicle before his body decides that if it is indeed a matter of survival—of fight and flight—then there's no time to be digesting food and it might as well empty its stomach.

Bent over the toilet bowl, racked by the heaving in his belly, he waits for the spasms to pass.

Why did the riot police pick me out? he thinks. *If they're coming after me, does that mean that the local force is corrupted by the Forty-Nine? Probably. And if that's right, then it means they already know I'm here. Someone in the company must have tipped them off.*

His stomach lurches again, and he leans over the bowl, but there's no more to come. His right ankle feels pretty sore now too, and he can feel his shin bleeding. *So many people out to get me*, he thinks. *So much that I don't understand yet.*

For a moment he feels small, terribly alone, wishing that Zamora was there beside him, the betrayal of the Mysterium rebirth forgotten. *Shouldn't have been cross with him, he's doing his best.* But why so many secrets all the time?

"The past reaches forward to the present," Darko used to say. "Whatever happened back there grabs hold of us here." But where did this story start? With the fire? With the sabotaged water torture cell? Or before that, when Dad recruited the wrong person, the bad apple? Or when he formed the company? The older the story, the harder it will be to fathom.

Danny gets to his feet uncertainly. He reaches into his pocket for his phone—but it's not there! Just that stupid carabiner. *Must have dropped it climbing the tower—or when I tripped and the devil caught me.*

He swears, kicking the toilet door in frustration. The cut on his shin throbs on the impact.

Planting his right foot on the edge of the basin, he rolls up the denim of his pant leg. Quite a lot of blood, seeping from a long gouge there. With a wet paper towel he cleans the wound and then ties another paper towel loosely around it. Cuts and bruises are no excuses—that always used to be the motto of the Mysterium's performers. What they dreaded were the turned ankles, separated shoulders, spinal injuries: the kinds of things that put you on crutches, threatened your career. To a man and woman everyone dreaded that—the thought that they might have to get a normal job! So wipe away a cut. Forget it.

He douses his face with cold water—over and over again—then rinses out his mouth, before planting both hands on the edge of the basin. He stares deeply into his own reflection. One green eye, one brown, both lit with determination—twin fires still burning.

Danny forces himself to smile at his reflection in the mirror, trying to chase away the fear and anxiety he sees reflected there. However deep and old the story is, he's going to find out what's happening. Find out who is the traitor in, or near, the Mysterium.

And maybe I'll even get the chance to punch that lion right on the nose.

10

WHY YOU CAN'T LEAVE IT TO AMATEURS

Not far away, La Loca is making her way down one of the darkest alleys. She takes off her lime-green coat and turns it inside out—a quick disguise as she pulls the now black garment back over her shoulders. She runs her hand thoughtfully across her close-cropped hair.

Two minutes earlier she has seen, high overhead, Danny's fleeting, dark figure, leaping the gap, arms and legs spread-eagled as he braced for landing. Then he was gone.

Not bad, she thinks. *Not bad*. The boy gave those goons the slip when it looked like they had him cornered. Resourceful. Brave too. Perhaps now she can see why the Forty-Nine have brought her in to do the job. If she's honest, it's sometimes harder to pull off the hit if you respect your target. Harder, but it makes you more determined—and she doesn't often respect the people she kills.

She pulls a phone from her pocket, hits a contact, and waits. An indistinct answer in Spanish, slightly hesitant.

"Your boys messed up," she says in English.

"What?"

"Amateurs. So I will do it now. Call everyone else off. I don't want anyone in my way unless I give an order. Understand me?"

"Of course."

"I pull the strings. I'm in control."

She punches the *End Call* icon and walks briskly away, past the people lining the alleyway beside the Picasso museum.

A plan is forming in her mind. A bit of a game, you might say. Might as well make this a decent challenge, give the young man something to work against. In the end she will snuff out his life, but it may as well be an entertaining few days and not just a run-of-the-mill hit. Nestled next to her own phone is the one she pickpocketed from the boy on the packed Ramblas. Lucky bumping into them like that!

She remembers the black cat she had when she was a girl. The thing had a mean streak that would show without warning, lighting its dull copper eyes with sudden mischief and malice.

One day it brought a mouse into their kitchen, still alive, twitching frantically in the cat's jaws. Then, for what seemed like an hour or more, the cat would drop the mouse, trap its tail just as it sensed freedom, let it run, then pounce across the kitchen and catch it again. Finally, as if growing bored, the cat struck decisively and killed the animal with a single flick of the paw, spattering blood on the white tiles.

Awful—but thrilling too.

ACT TWO

REMEMBERING THINGS THAT ARE PAST
IS NOT THE SAME AS REMEMBERING
THINGS AS THEY WERE.

—*Proust*

11

WHY DAD THREW
THE BOOK

An hour passes.

In the little park beside the Sagrada Familia, hidden in a slab of shadow under a tree, Danny cautiously studies the lay of the land.

He's made his way back, retracing his steps as best he could—through the square where the tower wobbled into the sky, up Las Ramblas, past the restless fountains of Plaça de Catalunya—hoping to find Zamora, eyes peeled, senses on full alert for those black helmets. But not a trace of the Major, or Danny's phone, or the police, to be seen.

If there's no sign of Zamora in the next five minutes, Danny thinks, *I'll make a dash for the back entrance and find Rosa.*

The blood has congealed on his leg, and his shin is throbbing. Parakeets screech green flashes overhead. The line for the cathedral is growing longer and longer, while tour buses rumble out fumes, engines idling. Not a policeman in sight—and certainly no one who looks like a member of an international criminal organization. But then they wouldn't, would they?

The rough bark of the pine tree bites into his back. *Need to plan a bit more*, he thinks. *Stop simply reacting to events.*

So break it down—use Dad's "atomic method" to split things into particles and then start to work through them one by one. The overarching question is too hazy to grasp, too vague: *What's going on here in Barcelona?* Need to list every part of it. *Why did the police come after me? Who can be trusted in the company?*

I mustn't take my eye off the older stuff either, he thinks. *It all must go together. The past might give clues to the present—and vice versa . . .*

On the way back to the cathedral he decided to ask Laura to send him copies of the coded entries in Dad's Escape Book. They must matter. In his mind's eye he can see the last few pages. He gazed at them so often—those long, gloomy afternoons at

Ballstone—that he can remember where the coded passages fell among the more humdrum entries and to-do lists. Strings of numbers, urgently underlined, the pencil scoring the paper, and asterisks planted before and after them. But the codes themselves are blurred and impossible to recall. *Wish I'd listened more when Dad went on about his memory techniques*, Danny thinks. *All the tricks he used to do in his earlier career on the cabaret circuit.*

How Dad loved that stuff. Mnemonics, memory games, and codes and ciphers too. He'd show Danny simple ones like pigpen and then demonstrate how they could be made more difficult with a keyword. Danny remembers the delight he felt when, as a young boy, he cracked a message that had been left lying around the trailer for him to find. How annoying it was when the decoded communication simply read: *Your mission, should you choose to accept it: tidy your end of the trailer,* and not some piece of exotic information like the whereabouts of a treasure hoard.

He used to nag for a "real adventure" with "proper clues"—but Dad, exhausted from grappling with the finances of the company or a disastrous rehearsal, would shake his head and slump on one of the couches, plucking a book from the shelf overhead, snapping, *Not now, Danny. I'm shattered.* And then he would be gone, buried in a well-thumbed paperback, leaving Danny wishing for a brother or sister or at least some friends his own age in the company.

And I'm still alone, Danny thinks.

He glances at his watch. The five minutes are nearly up.

Then—with a rush of relief—he sees Zamora getting out of a taxi. The Major looks none the worse for his brush with the law, his familiar bustling energy propelling him from the cab. But there's a stranger with him now, a powerfully built man who towers over the dwarf. They both look quickly up and down the street—Zamora throwing his arms up in frustration or disappointment—then the big man puts a hand on his shoulder. They both stride toward the main door of the cathedral, the dwarf taking two and a half steps for every one of his companion.

Danny bursts from the shadow and nips across the road, dodging between the beggars and tourists. "Major! I'm here!"

Zamora turns around, the lines on his forehead smoothing as his own relief hits. "Danny! *Madre mia.* I was worried stupid. You're OK?"

"Yep." Danny nods, but his eyes have slipped to the Major's companion, who is listening intently. *Perhaps better to keep my cards close to my chest*, he thinks. *Don't reveal my hand yet.*

The man's built like a bear, with strong arms, strong shoulders. An open, wide face, a nose like the prow of a ship. He's zipped up tight in an expensive, brown leather jacket. The Major spots Danny's uncertainty.

"Ah. Do you remember Javier Luis? Javier's booking us here."

"You won't remember me," the man says in a thick Spanish accent, "but I remember you." He holds out a spade of a hand, enveloping Danny's and shaking it firmly. "You all OK? Lost those dogs?"

"Yes. *Gracias.*"

Javier returns his gaze. There's something reassuring in his strength, and it makes the tension that's been held in Danny's shoulders soften.

"Let's get out of sight," Zamora says and jerks his head toward the park beyond. "Tell me what happened when we're safely up in Javier's place. Just across the road. We need to do some research . . . and Jav has some useful contacts—from our old days here together."

The other man smiles, eyes flicking away, as if remembering something. But there's an edge to the memory, you can see that. Something sad or dark, its force blunted by time but still pulling away at the corners of his mouth. It resonates powerfully enough that Danny feels it tighten his own face, and as they go back through the shadowed park, a shiver ripples across his skin.

12

WHY NEPHEWS CAN BE BAD FOR YOUR HEALTH

Javier's grand apartment looks directly onto the mountainous form of the Sagrada.

Danny, still recovering from the shock and effort of the chase, sits in the window, his eyes drawn to the vertigo-inducing towers, the cranes floating in the air above even them. How high? It would make an incredible wire walk. But even with his head for heights, he feels his knees weaken at the thought.

Way up there, floating against the curling clouds, he can just make out the cabs of the crane operators: remote aerial boxes inhabited by tiny figures. They might as well be astronauts working on some remote space station, an impossible drop to the earth under their feet.

Behind him, Zamora and Javier are crouched over a laptop, tapping out e-mails, whispering to each other in a mix of Catalan and standard Spanish. Every now and then a word pops out: *Danny, policia, Tibidabo.* —They would look ridiculous together, these two—a dwarf and a half-giant—if it wasn't for the concern holding their faces tight. You can tell that they know each other really well: shoulders touching, heads nodding in agreement. Strange that Danny can't even remember *hearing* about Javier. *If they go so far back, then surely I'd have seen him around the Mysterium from time to time—especially on Spanish tours?*

Zamora coughs and shuts the lid of the laptop.

"Well?" Danny asks, eager to know what they've discovered but fearing the answer at the same time.

"Javier's sure that those men—at least the ones who came after you and me—are part of a riot squad that's got a bad reputation for corruption—"

"So that means one thing," Danny cuts in, feeling the nausea returning to catch his throat—but a weird kind of thrill too. "It must mean that the Forty-Nine put them onto us."

"We don't know that for sure, do we?" Zamora says. "All we know is that someone killed some poor guy and burnt dots on his back—"

"But forty-nine of them! They must be here. In Barcelona."

Javier shakes his head. "I have heard . . . the rumors. But I always took them with a pinch of—salt? Didn't take what I heard that seriously. And I was only ever a very small fish in a very big and murky sea."

Danny looks hard at the Catalan. "We *can* trust Javier, can't we, Major?" he says, without taking his eyes off him.

"Of course!" Zamora splutters, genuinely affronted. "Javier and I were knocking around this town before you were even born, Mister Danny. Before the Olympics came here. We've had our fair share of problems—swam shark-infested waters, you might say—but I'd trust him with my life."

Javier's still returning Danny's gaze. No reaction from the man apart from a shrug, as if he's indifferent to the suspicion. Or used to it. "It seems to me," he says, "that now we have to take these rumors a bit more seriously, no?"

Danny's working hard at the little tells—the tiny, uncontrolled pieces of body—coming from the man opposite. Javier's hands are half-clenched. Certainly tension there. But the eyes are blinking at normal speed. He's not glancing away at the vital moments. Either he's as trustworthy as the Major thinks—or very good at hiding any lies or deception.

I'll trust him, Danny thinks. *Trust the Major's judgment.* "If the Forty-Nine *are* here, then someone's tipped them off. Only a handful of people know I'm in Barcelona, so there are only a few suspects—once we cross some of the company off the list."

"*Some* of them?!" Zamora chokes. "*All* of them, I would say, Mister Danny."

Danny shakes his head firmly. It's the moment to play his trump card. He's been guarding the information ever since the escape in Hong Kong, but now he needs to convince Zamora—and Javier—quickly. No point in holding on to it until the game's over!

"I remembered something when I was struggling out of the freezer back in Hong Kong. Something from the week just before the fire. I think being in the same situation as Dad somehow triggered it."

"We've been over this—"

"But I'd forgotten something. That night of the accident, I saw that one of the Klowns had a smear of paint on his knee."

"I don't see—"

"Billy and Dad had painted the water cell the night before and left it to dry. But one of the Klowns obviously had paint on his knee. Probably kneeling on top of the cell—maybe to plug the padlocks or something like that."

"Now hold on, Mister Danny, that's a *very* serious allegation—"

"I know it is!" Danny snaps impatiently. He's always thought that Zamora saw him as an equal, didn't see him as just a kid. But now he's frustrated that the Major is slow to agree with his suspicions. Maybe he's just like the rest of them.

"There's something else. Aki and Joey looked at each other in a funny way when I turned up this morning. Like they weren't that pleased to see me—"

"They always look odd," Zamora says. "And anyway why would they want to hurt Harry and Lily? Doesn't make sense."

Javier has been watching the exchange closely. "Perhaps their involvement was not direct. Perhaps one of them is a messenger for the bad guys, no? You told me yourself, Zamora, these Klowns have a lot of baggage. Debts. *Prob-lem-as!*"

Zamora slumps down on the edge of a coffee table and scratches his head. "And you're sure about this, Danny? I mean, you *were* under a lot of stress and—"

"I'm sure."

"So which Klown, then?"

"They were wearing their skull masks. Aki or Joey. Don't think it was someone as big as Bjorn."

Zamora gets back to his feet and puts his powerful hands on Danny's shoulders. "One thing's for sure. If the Forty-Nine know you're here and are out to get you, then I should put you on the first flight home. Or get Laura to come and fetch you right now."

"No!" Danny's voice is controlled, but there's force in it—all the force he can muster. "I won't go. I'm not going to give this up now. I want to find out why Mum and Dad were killed. My best chance of doing that is right here. Right now."

There's silence for a moment. Outside a crane is stirring the clouds with its bright yellow jib, another block of stone swinging into position high up on the cathedral towers.

"Please, Major."

To Danny's surprise it is Javier who lends his support. "Zamora, if the Forty-Nine are as real as Danny thinks, then nowhere is safe. Not here, not

England, not even the frozen *Polo Norte*. But here we can get our own help. Security from my clubs or some of the old gang."

The Major puffs out his cheeks, undecided.

Javier presses his point. "We can keep Danny safe *here*. This is home ground, no?"

And Danny sees the little tilt of Zamora's head, the one he knows means, *OK, you win*.

"*Vale*. No point worrying Laura about what's already done, I suppose. And I'm sure she'll be here soon enough."

Danny clenches his fists. It's a little victory.

"But you do as I say—" the Major adds.

Danny nods, getting to his feet. "I need to speak to Laura and get her to send me some scans of the last few pages in Dad's Escape Book. It's important."

———————————

When his aunt's face appears on the Skype screen, it's hard to tell which emotion has the upper hand. Relief and anger are fighting each other for control—but she takes a deep breath and puffs the hair out of her eyes like always.

"You, Danny Boy, have taken years off my life. Nephews should have a government health warning tattooed on them."

Danny makes his own features relax—especially the eyes—and smiles back, trying to reassure her. Trying to reassure himself. "I'm sorry, Aunt Laura. I just *had* to—"

She holds up a hand. "Listen! Ricard e-mailed me this morning. He's had evidence from an informer that the Forty-Nine are way more than a rumor after all. Quite a bit more. I'm going to have to come and get you."

"But—"

So it's real. Any doubts swept away. He feels his shoulders tightening, his heart bumping up its rhythm again.

"No arguments. You'll be OK there with Zamora until tomorrow evening or the day after. Then we're going to a safe house in the remotest bit of country-side I can find."

"But the Mysterium—"

"Blast the bleeding show, Danny. I'm talking about your life here. God only knows why they've got it in for you, but Ricard says the boss of the Forty-Nine, the one they call Center, personally wants to see you 'pay.' For what and why I don't know, but we have to take it *very* seriously."

Now that he's spoken out against the Klowns, now that Laura has confirmed his worst suspicions, Danny feels vulnerable, as if someone has drawn a target on his back. He glances out of the window. Cranes, clouds. Nothing more. Kwan's whispered words—"my boss wants you dead"—float back to him with renewed impact. He swallows hard, tries to keep his composure.

The main thing is to win some extra time here. *I'll play along*, he thinks, *even if I've no intention whatsoever of boarding a plane for England—at least until the storm has played out.* If you give way in a struggle, it can buy you some slack, enough time, while the other person thinks they've won.

"Whatever you think, Aunt Laura," he says, dropping his shoulders, looking dejected.

"Good lad. Don't be afraid."

"Could you do me a favor?"

"Probably."

"In my desk are Dad's old notes. They're in a big hardback notebook. Could you get that out and scan the last few pages and e-mail them to Zamora? Today?"

"Can't it wait?!"

"Do that—and I'll do whatever you say." He pauses for emphasis. "It'll stop me from being afraid."

Laura sighs. "I'll do my best. I can't promise, though. I've got other problems to sort. My lawyer says he's had a weird phone call from the police. Some trial in Rome. If it rains, it pours . . ."

"Please? Then I'll get on the plane without a fuss."

Laura sighs. "OK. Take really good care for now. Speak later." She reaches out to press the button to hang up, and the screen goes dark.

Javier slowly nods his approval as Danny closes the laptop. "You were playing her, weren't you? To get what you wanted?"

Embarrassed, Danny looks away, avoiding Javier's gaze.

"We all have to do that at times," the tall man says. "Your papa could wrap people round his finger when he wanted."

"You knew him?" Danny asks uncertainly, wondering if Javier is about to reveal another flaw of Dad's character.

"*Si, si.* And I knew you too, Danny. But you were *very* small. Come and have a look at this."

He leads the way into the high-ceilinged dining room. Two young children, a boy and a girl not much more than five or six, are having their lunch, jabbering away between mouthfuls.

"My kids," Javier says proudly, "Paco and Lucia." The children look up and beam at their father.

"But this is what I want to show you."

Dominating the far wall is a massive, ornately framed photograph.

"You might recognize one or two people," Javier says.

The top half of the image smolders in rich, dark shadows. Below that, dramatically lit and posed, are an array of familiar figures. From left to right: a younger Javier, standing with an antique box camera on a tripod, gazing at the viewer, the shutter release held in his hand. Next to him, Izzy and Beatrice—beautiful in their ostrich-feathered "black angel" costumes—crouch either side of a young, dark-haired boy, maybe no more than three years old.

Next to the Aerialisques stands the unmistakable form of Major Zamora, his face calm, composed. Another dwarf, a woman, stands by his side, gazing in admiration. A dog—presumably Herzog, his hair still more black than gray—is curled at the boy's feet.

Danny approaches the photograph, brings his finger close to the glass, to the figure of the young boy. It's hard to make out the eye color, but there's no mistaking the intensity of the gaze.

"It's me, isn't it?" he says quietly.

Javier nods. "Eight or nine years ago."

"I don't remember."

In the shadows behind stand Rosa and Jimmy Torrini—both looking quite a bit younger—and silhouetted in a brightly lit doorway at the back, another figure seems to be either joining or leaving the group.

"It's based on a painting by Velázquez," Javier says. "The original work showed the Spanish court watching the artist paint the king and queen. It took me all day to work out the angles to match things up. Can you see the king and queen? The real subjects of the picture? I'll give you a clue . . ."

But Danny has already spotted them. Dimly reflected in a mirror at the back of the room hover the ghostlike faces of Dad and Mum. Not in the picture and in it at the same time.

"What do you think?" Javier says, coming to stand beside Danny and putting a hand on his shoulder.

But Danny can't respond. He's busy stuffing emotion back down inside. Something so mysterious, so moving about it. Like a kind of prophecy—that they would be gone but still hanging around, still watching him. He takes the air deep into his lungs, and blows out long and hard.

"Who's that other dwarf?"

"Gala," a voice says behind him. Zamora has come in quietly and is gazing up at the photograph. "We were an item for a while. But it didn't work out."

"I don't remember her, either."

"You were very small," Zamora says, perhaps eager to shift the subject. "Javier did an amazing job, no? I'd always wanted us to re-create it somehow—in an act maybe. Thing about Velázquez, he was the first artist to paint us dwarves as real people. Not just pets or freaks. Bless him."

Danny nods, but his gaze is fixed on Mum and Dad's reflected faces, smiling from out of their perpetual half-light.

"Come on, *amigo*," Zamora says gently. "I've got to rehearse."

A dark-haired woman comes into the room carrying a pot of coffee. The early afternoon light reflects off it, picking out care-worn lines around her eyes. No hiding the tension there, even as she forces a smile.

"And this is Lope. My wife," Javier says. He gives her a kiss on the cheek. "Sorry, *cariño*. We've got to go."

The woman sets the pot down, takes a folded piece of paper from her pocket, and presses it into Javier's hand.

"*Una comunicación*," she murmurs, and very briefly Danny catches the unmistakable glint of fear in her dark eyes.

Javier glances at the note, flinches almost imperceptibly, and then stuffs it in his own jacket pocket. "If anyone else calls, tell them I'm out of town."

"Everything is OK though?" Lope asks.

"All fine," he says. And then gives her an extra kiss. "All fine."

But clearly it isn't. Danny can tell that easily enough. Lope squeezes Javier's hand very hard and then turns quickly away.

That look in Lope's eyes stays with Danny. It's so raw that for a moment it blocks everything else out.

On the stairs he turns to Javier.

"Were you in the Mysterium too?"

Zamora snorts at that. "He should have been. Isn't that right, *amigo*? Then you wouldn't have gone to prison."

"Prison? What for?" Danny asks, surprised.

"Oh," Javier says, slinging his jacket over his shoulder. "Murder. Among other things."

13

WHY THE SNAKE SWALLOWED ITS TAIL

Deep in thought, Danny follows the Major and his friend across the park, up the cathedral steps, through the interior of the Sagrada. How casually Javier tossed "murder" into the conversation, like you'd mention an unexceptional vacation. He wants to like Javier—in fact he already does—but the mention of that word, and the electric look that passed between him and his wife, seem to have upped the stakes yet again. *Just another thing to worry about,* Danny thinks as they slip through the forest of stone pillars toward the far end of the cathedral.

Rosa is waiting for them. She's standing just outside the temporary screen in a pool of green light, arms folded, her boot tapping the flagstones. "I said lunchtime," she snaps. "We're going to mess up, Zamora—"

She stops mid-flow and points at Danny's shin. The blood is smudging through the denim in dark patches. "What happened to you, *bello*?"

"I . . . um . . . I fell over on Las Ramblas."

Rosa sighs a long breath. "Maria's just redone her first aid training. She'll fix you up." She glances at their companion. "*Hola*, Javier. We're in a mess! I wish I still smoked."

She leads them through the plastic curtaining into the performance space. But Danny hangs back, tugging at Zamora's sleeve. "Javier killed someone?!"

The Major shakes his head. "Self-defense. It was him or the other man. The conviction was reduced to manslaughter. Javier's a good man."

Zamora glances around him. "But let's keep this morning—and the rest—to ourselves for now. Until we're sure what's going on."

Danny nods. *That's a good strategy*, he thinks. *See if any of the company look surprised to see me walk back in, safe and sound. But I think I'll keep an open mind about Javier. At least for now.*

He sets his shoulders, tries to push away the

morning and its developments, and slips through the screen . . .

. . . and catches his breath.

The setup looks amazing now, with more silks tumbling from the scaffolding and the great starry field of the old Mysterium backdrop pulled high across the far windows. Tiny spotlights splay across the rigging, gently revolving, while tall columns of purple light shine into the vast space of the nave, piercing the dry ice and smoke. Suddenly the past is even closer. *Can almost feel it now*, Danny thinks, *and not just see it. So close . . .*

But there's a job to do. He shoves the rising emotion back down inside and scrutinizes the company, looking for any little hint of surprise—or shock, or anger even—that may be the only clue he needs.

The safety net has been dragged across the arena, and above their heads, Bjorn is swinging on the catcher's bar, hanging by his knees, arms trailing lazy arcs through the air. He sees Danny and waves a chalk-whitened palm, an upside-down smile spreading on his face.

"OK, let's go," Rosa barks, clapping her hands. "First part of the flyer routine. Come on, boys!"

Billy starts up the chiming distorted chords of

"*Expressway to Your Skull,*" and Maria, sitting beside him, takes up her cello.

"You didn't tell me you'd hurt yourself," Zamora shouts over the thump of the music.

"It's OK." Danny shrugs the concern away, eager to watch the reaction to his reappearance.

He leans back against a rigging support, eyes swiveling from one Mysterium artist to the other. Billy and Maria are lost in the music, oblivious to anything else. Darko is sitting on a flight case, absorbed in a phone conversation, his eyes shut as he strains to hear the person at the other end. Frankie is holding one end of a lunge rope and gazing up into the vaulted ceiling. The only company member who really seems interested in him is Herzog, who pads over now, tail wagging, before slumping down at Danny's feet. Danny bends down to stroke Herzog's shaggy head, and it helps to steady his nerves.

What about the other two Klowns?

Aki and Joey stand ready on their platforms, confident—looking for all the world like a couple of cocky parrots, their spiked hair glowing in the lights. Bjorn makes his bar swing harder and, at the top of the next swing, claps his hands. Joey, poised above him, swan dives toward the net, falling for a moment—but perfectly timed, so his hands and Bjorn's grip each other firmly. He swings two big arcs and then, in one long somersault, pivots across the gap and catches the bar on the far side. That's the cue for Aki to go.

But then, glancing down, Aki's eyes seem to pick out Danny, and he hesitates. It's just a fraction, but it throws off his timing, and so, when he releases, flying out through the spotlights, his fingers just clip Bjorn's arm.

And then he goes tumbling down, a cry of anguish piercing the music, ragdoll arms and legs in a mess as he lands in the safety net.

Was that it? Was that the reaction I was looking for? Danny wonders, heart thumping. It wasn't much—but something messed up the timing. He stares at the Klown, who is now struggling to free himself from the net.

Rosa is shaking her head. Billy and Maria change their riff into broken pieces, and Maria laughs sarcastically into her microphone—the way they normally cover a fall. Darko comes over, pulling a face, shoving his phone into his pocket.

"Aki's still not in top form, Rosa." He glances at Danny. "What would your old papa say, Danny?

Imbeciles! I'm surrounded by imbeciles." It's a pretty good impression of Dad's rumbling voice, the buried Welsh accent. But the mimicry jars.

"For God's sake, Darko," Zamora says.

"If he's brave enough to be here, then he can cope with that," Darko says and pats Danny firmly on the back. "Isn't that right?"

But Danny's eyes are so intent on seeking out the Klowns that the remark has flown over his head. Joey is looking down, leaning out, left leg poised on the takeoff board, holding on by one hand, grinning at his fallen companion. His gaze flips to Danny.

Don't look away, Danny thinks. *Don't show you're afraid.*

"You put him off, Daniel!" the Frenchman calls down. And laughs again through his mask. "But then everything does this week!"

"Let's break," Rosa shouts. "Five minutes. And Maria, can you fix Danny's leg up before he bleeds all over the cathedral floor?"

Joey grins, balances on the takeoff board, and then dead falls to the net below.

Maria wheels out the first aid kit, a silver flight case with a large red cross plastered on it and the stenciled words: *MYSTERIUM HOSPITAL.* She crouches down next to Danny, rolls up his pant leg, and winces. There's blood still oozing from the wound.

"Jeez, Danny—how did you do that? It might need a stitch or two."

"OK," he says, but seeing the dark blood oozing from the wound, he suddenly feels tiredness sweeping up to catch him, and his body sags.

Maria sits up straight and looks him in the eye. "Maybe it's too much. To come back, I mean, and your folks not to be here . . ." Her voice trails away uncertainly. Then her face brightens. "Hey, wanna see my new tattoo?"

She lifts her vest up, turning around. And there, coiled on her lower back, is a snake, wrapped in coiling flame, turning around to bite its own tail, looped in a figure eight. The sign for infinity.

"It's called an ouroboros. Cool, huh? To show how things just keep going and going. No matter what . . . um . . . happens . . ."

"Dad used to leave that sign for Mum, when they were first getting together. Bent twigs or scraped in the frost," Danny says, glad to have a good memory triggered. Mum always used to say how wonderful it was to see a sign of their love displayed in the open—maybe traced in the condensation on a café window—yet still hidden if you didn't know how to read it.

"We all miss them, Danny," Maria says. Again, she pauses, unsure if she has said too much.

Danny looks down at his bloodied shin, doing his best to force a smile. Maybe Maria can add another piece to the puzzle. It's worth asking everyone.

"Maria, do you remember that last day? The day of the fire?"

Maria sighs. "It was just *too* horrible, Danny. I dunno . . ."

She's tiptoeing around something. Avoiding. You can see it by the way her eyes skip away and back again. But something she wants to get out of her system.

"Tell me," he says—and taps her arm as he says it, just right, on the point on the forearm that Dad said helped people to let things go. He obviously gets it right, because Maria sighs. "Oh, God forgive me. It's just that I told your Dad to go and get stuffed that afternoon. Much, *much* worse actually. Told him to drop dead, with a few bad words around it. He could be such a sod, some days, you know? It's the last thing I said to him. Jeez, I feel *soooo* bad about it."

There are tears in her eyes. It's painful to hear something critical about Dad again. Danny glances away. *But nothing more sinister there*, he thinks, *I'm sure about that.*

"God. I should be looking after you," Maria says, pulling herself together. "What about these stitches?"

"I can cope."

"This might sting." She cleans the wounds with antiseptic wipes, and Danny winces in spite of himself. But by the time Maria has taken a sterile needle from a pack, carefully eyed the thread—tongue out in concentration—and bent to his shin, his mind is so busy that he barely notices the stitches going in.

His eyes are roving the performance area again, straining to see what the others are doing.

Darko's flinging knives at his target board. They flash in the gloom and *thunk* into the wood, barely a finger's width from the chalked outline of a person. Rosa and the Aerialisques are leafing through a running order, faces serious, concentrated.

Beyond them, Joey and Aki are locked tight in conversation. They glance in his direction—and then quickly away again.

Am I projecting it, Danny thinks, *or is that the look and reaction of guilt?*

14

WHY HAPPINESS IS A WARM GUN

About half a mile away—tucked in the warren-like backstreets of the Raval district—La Loca is bent over a brilliantly lit workbench.

Music plays quietly in the background—a lively rhythm that sets her right foot tapping. She hums under her breath and bends to the task in hand.

There's a small timer device, and that has to be linked to the dead man's phone so that it can be activated remotely. Next to that on the bench is the plastic explosive—a cellophane-wrapped package, off-white in color. More than enough to do the job, she thinks, but then it might as well look spectacular, and she's covering the expense anyway. Once all that is done, there's the heavy-duty magnet to fit to the strap of the shoulder bag. And then, blammo!

The boy's phone next to it: she'll change the SIM, then let him have it back!

She whistles under her breath as she works away with skilled, controlled fingers, joins in with the chorus of the song playing in the background. *"Happiness is a warm gun. Happiness . . ."*

Beyond the reach of the desk lamp looms her filing cabinet. In it, neatly detailed, precisely and chronologically organized, forever at rest, are her victims. A file for every name she has erased from the book of life over the years. Nobody has ever looked into the files and lived. And nobody ever will.

It is a mystery to her why the name La Loca has stuck. Her actions are precisely the opposite. Calculated, deliberate, rational. Her services exchanged for the appropriate fee. No details left to chance and no failures. You call in La Loca—at a very high price—when you want to be sure of getting something done.

The iron hisses and bubbles molten metal—solder—onto the two wires that must be joined. She breathes in the acrid fumes and holds them in her lungs for a moment.

On the workbench next to her is a printout of an e-mail from her client.

Essential to take this chance. Opponents have been tipped off. Leak has been liquidated but damage done. Local head 38 and operatives informed and standing by while you bring matters to a conclusion.

Instead of a signature, there's a neat grid of forty-nine dots. At the dead heart of the pattern a thick red circle marks the central dot. A bull's-eye.

Center.

15

WHY THE STEW WOULDN'T GO DOWN

The day is fading. The Klowns and Aerialisques are packing up after their part of the rehearsal. Faces are relaxing, backs being patted. There's rather more of the atmosphere of the old days. But still Danny's tense, expectant.

He's spent the time looking for clues in the reactions and movements of the company, but nothing more has leapt to attention.

And still there's a chunk of something raw, emotional, lodged at the bottom of his throat. Javier's mysterious photograph has stirred powerful feelings, and now they want to come jumping up out of his mouth. He swallows hard, trying to force them down.

Now that darkness is falling, the transformation of the Mysterium's performance area is complete—as if the great tent has been pitched and they're once again under its hemisphere. All you can see are the familiar props, the rigging, the trapeze and cloud swings, the star-filled backdrop with its miniature lights smoldering behind, galaxies and constellations pulsing in and out of existence. There's Orion again, high up. Can it be only yesterday he was watching the starry hunter stalking over the Parisian grave-yard? Is it really less than two years since he last watched Mum and Dad performing in this dramatic space? The knot in his throat tightens.

Maria is flying through the air on her cloud swing, turning circles, her hair and tattoos spin-ning, picked bright in a beam. The golden loop of the ouroboros flashes on her back. It stops Danny short. Despite the rush of his thoughts, the anxiety, a sight like this thrills you, lifts your heart, reminds you it's good to be alive. Good to be in the business of reminding *others* of that fact.

Rosa and Zamora come over to join him.

"What do you know?" the ringmistress smiles. "We actually got through a complete tech run without a mess-up. We've got one bit still to do, though . . ."

She nods pointedly at Zamora's red cannon crouching to one side, resting on its carefully measured marks, black gaffer tape crosses on the floor.

"But chow time first," Rosa says, stretching. "You hungry, *bello*?"

"Yes. Very," Danny says, but in truth, he's worried that he's about to be sick again. *Something definitely doesn't feel right. Maybe I'm coming down with a bug?*

"I've made my old standby. *Ri-bol-lita!*"

The company members assemble around a long trestle table in a back room. Aki moves to sit at the head, but Zamora blocks him off with a strong arm. "Let's give Danny the place of honor today. To show how glad we *all* are to see him. He's earned it."

Murmurs of assent come from the company. Danny tries to push away the embarrassment at suddenly being the center of attention, grateful for Zamora's gesture, but wishing he could just sit and watch quietly from the side, wait for the nausea to ease down at least.

Need to keep alert, he thinks. *Need to keep my eyes soft and scan for any reaction or posture that seems false.* Do the Klowns, for example, seem less than enthusiastic as a chorus of "Cheers," "*Salud*," "*Santé*" rises from the table and glasses are raised in his direction?

Rosa is heaving a huge pot of stew onto the table and starting to ladle out bowls brimful of *ribollita*.

"I hope you still like this, *bello*. You always used to back when—when you were younger."

"How's your shin, Danny?" Maria calls from the other end of the table.

"Fine, thanks," he says, trying to sound bright, but the cloying, choking sensation is getting worse in his throat, eyes watering.

"Sounds like you were in the wars in Hong Kong too," Frankie Boom chips in from across the table. "What's the story?"

"Oh, let the lad eat," Zamora says hurriedly.

Danny looks down into the stew, trailing his spoon in the bowl, wondering what he should say— if he can indeed say anything.

"I used some stuff Dad taught me . . ." he stumbles. The *ribollita* is still too hot, but the herby smells coiling up from his bowl are jogging away at his memory now, pushing his mind back, back . . .

"I'm still not clear how you ended up on that roof anyway," Joey pushes.

Danny lifts a spoonful of the rich, aromatic stew to his lips, blows on it, takes a sip. And then something very weird happens.

It's as if the food is laced with a powerful drug.

As the distinctive flavor hits his taste buds, time seems to hang, to freeze, the table before him to soften, dissolve, and the faces around him to blur. That great mass of whatever that has been lodged in his stomach comes bolting up into his mouth, into his nose, unlocking—at long last—a tidal wave of memory and grief.

It all comes rushing back in that one moment—countless other meals like this, sitting around the communal table, bottles of wine being passed, someone strumming a guitar, pumping an accordion. Laughter, lively talk, awkward silences, crossed words, swearing, storytelling—all accompanied by plate after plate of Rosa's cooking. Sometimes still in costume, face paint daubed on their faces, sometimes relaxed in jeans and T-shirts. Gossiping, joke telling, flirting, exchanging memories, but above all else, laughing.

Often they sat under the open starry night, the white table glowing, maybe a Klown or two stumbling around, hand-launching fireworks that burst over their heads and made even more laughter as the rocket sticks came clattering back down through the trees or even onto the table. The wild laughter and energy . . . from before it all stopped dead and the lights went out and the charred remains of his home were scooped up and dropped unceremoniously into a truck and taken away to who knows where.

But it's more than that. The last time he had a bowl of *ribollita* was the night of the fire itself, and the remembered taste—so immediate and powerful—unlocks more of the story now . . .

He had been sitting in Rosa's caravan when they heard the alarm being raised, Darko's voice screaming, "FIRE! FIRE!" The taste of the stew was still in his mouth as he and Rosa stumbled through the falling snow and saw the flames coughing up heavy black smoke. He has blocked the full memory ever since, but now—rather than the fragments that normally haunt him—the whole scene comes rushing back. He remembers the company doing their best to extinguish the flames, remembers Herzog barking, Maria and Frankie discharging first one, then two, then three extinguishers hopefully, hopelessly, into the inferno, Zamora trying to brave the smoke and being pushed back, the Klowns arriving, staring at the flaming monster devouring Mum and Dad.

I remember. I remember, he thinks. The snow falling harder, almost choking it was so thick, and . . .

he was looking around for more help, for another extinguisher or even a fire engine, and everyone was there. And then someone screamed—Izzy or Beatrice—and Danny's attention was back on the fire and he was running toward the flames, determined to save them, but Zamora caught him and shouted, *No Danny, no. You can't*. And held him back as the fire raged and raged . . .

Consuming itself, then finally dying as the howling fire engines arrived.

———————————

Dimly he is aware of voices now. Someone—Rosa?—is asking if he is all right, if something has gone down the wrong way. But it's as if he can't see this present moment—just fire and snow—and, beyond that, all those other countless moments that lie in the past, hundreds of thousands of them, the wild, unfurling drama of the Mysterium.

And all of the grief he has held in check for so long wells up and bursts in his chest.

It rocks his body and his shoulders are shaking and he's gasping for breath, trying to get his head up, trying to get air. Can't control it. Not anymore . . .

"*Carajo*! Give the boy some air," Zamora says. "Come on, Danny. Let it out . . ."

Danny breathes deeply, trying to calm the shudders passing through him. It feels as if something is making his arms and legs jump and twitch. Beyond his control. Teeth chattering. Cold gripping him. But, at the same time, it feels like there's a weight releasing off his chest, the emotion jumping free and running through his system.

Rosa takes off her jacket and puts it over his shoulders. "*Bello*. It's OK. It's OK."

The shockwaves are passing now, subsiding. He's aware of hushed conversations around him.

It feels embarrassing to be going to pieces like this. And yet the breaking grief somehow feels good too, as if a wall has been pulled down and finally— *finally*—he can feel things again, feel the raw power of that night. Painful but vital. And there's more to that specific chain of memory, he thinks, more to remember about the fire, he's sure. *If I could just follow it through . . . Zamora held me back and I tried to break loose, but he was too strong, and I looked up into the endless snowfall and—*

But then a loud voice, brimful of energy, familiar, breaks the spell.

"Well, I'm here! Wasn't some clown supposed to flipping well meet me at the station?"

Can't be!

Danny's head jerks up, and his mouth falls open in astonishment.

"Sing Sing!"

She's standing in the doorway with a suitcase, her eyes sparkling behind her glasses. The surprise chases the last of Danny's shivering from him and he stands, his strength returning. In the same moment she spots him—and her face mirrors his own.

"What on earth are you doing here?" they both say as one.

Zamora is looking from one to another. Despite the intensity of the last few minutes, he's chuckling to himself.

"Ah yes, Mister Danny. Something else I've been meaning to tell you . . ."

16

WHY ZAMORA GOT FIRED FOR THE LAST TIME

The evening has fallen. Danny and Sing Sing sit on a stone bench, dwarfed in the vastness of the Sagrada's interior, the spiraling, gravity-defying stonework glowing all around them in the Mysterium's lights. Stairways corkscrew up the sides of the building into the towers. Through the windows you can make out the orange scaffolding clamped to the flanks of the cathedral and, beyond that, the bright yellow cranes piercing the night.

Sing Sing is taking it all in, a cup of coffee in her hands, watching the rest of the company gathering for a late "snagging" rehearsal away to their left.

The immediate shock and joy of reunion has lapsed into a moment of awkwardness. Danny feels pleased to see her—he's sure of that—but darkening the emotion is a mixture of unease and irritation that yet again secrets have been kept from him. Even during their brief time together in Hong Kong, he sensed the deep currents pulling at Sing Sing. Now he wonders just how much she has been hiding. What can she possibly be doing here?

She looks at him, then glances away at a stairway coiling into the shadows above.

"Crazy flipping place. But it's supercool for a venue." *She can't meet my eyes*, Danny thinks. Hasn't really done so for the last hour or so, not after that initial greeting. Like she's embarrassed, caught red-handed.

"You shouldn't have left. Not without coming to see me," he begins, feeling for the right tone, but the frustration all too obvious in his voice.

"Couldn't be helped," Sing Sing says briskly. "You were really out of it. And I had stuff to do."

"Like what?"

"Like personal stuff."

"To do with Charlie?"

"My own flippin' detective work."

"But what are you doing *here*?'

"I could ask the same thing," she says, jutting

out her chin. *It's almost like the first day we met,* Danny thinks. The armor's back on. Does what happened later in Hong Kong count for nothing?

"It was an emergency," he says, wondering how much he should share but keen to bridge the gap between them. When did Sing Sing know she would be coming here? When did she know the Mysterium was re-forming, for that matter? *Well, try and forget it,* he thinks. *I need her on my side, need to get her trust, bit by bit. If I'm totally honest, then there's a good chance she will be honest too . . .*

So, briefly, he gives her the facts: the forty-nine dots on the dead man's back, the chase by the riot police, his suspicions about the Klowns. Sing Sing listens quietly, attentively, nodding, then screws her face up in thought. "Sounds like you made a good move," she says at last. "Bet your aunt was mad, though!"

"She'll be OK. But what about you? Tell me why *you're* here."

Sing Sing sighs—a long, deflating sigh that carries more than just tiredness with it. Something sad? Heavier than that.

"I told you everything. It's only fair if you tell me," he says more firmly.

"Three reasons." She counts them off on her fingers. "Number one: need a flippin' change from Hong Kong. Bad memories. Number two: I'm following a clue or two of my own—"

"For Ricard?"

"No. For me. And number three: I'm looking for work and I've got an interview." A grin flickers on her face.

"In Barcelona?"

"Here. Right here. With the Mysterium."

She laughs at Danny's blank look of astonishment. "I told you I did my own tricks, right? Well, your friend Zamora mentioned they were scouting for new talent. Everything fell into place. Cremated Charlie, scattered his ashes in the harbor, and bought my ticket with the last of his money. And here I am! Homeless. Broke. I'm auditioning tomorrow."

How to respond to that? *Good for her,* he thinks, *but it should be ME auditioning. I belong here—and she just waltzes in!*

"What's your act?" he says flatly.

"It's a surprise! Here, hold my glasses."

She leaps up onto the bench, eyes bright. Then takes a breath and does a forward somersault onto the stone floor. From that she takes two running steps and goes cartwheeling away, two, three turns, into a punch somersault forward, landing in perfect splits.

Danny applauds quietly as she returns, still trying to push the jealousy from his mind but impressed all the same. She's the real deal.

"Acrobat?"

"Kinda."

Zamora is coming over with three sheets of paper in his hand. He flourishes them in the air.

"Laura's e-mailed those pages. She said she'll send more tomorrow when she's feeling less cross!"

That chases the envy away in a moment—and everything else. Danny takes them eagerly.

It's good to see Dad's powerful handwriting on the scans. But whereas before it seemed little more than a private game, now Dad's underlining, the asterisks marking the code, all read as rushed and urgent. Danny remembers that entry on the first page of the Escape Book—*You hold the key in your hands*—and realizes that those hands are shaking now ever so slightly.

"I'll leave them with you, Mister Danny. Unless you want to come and see me get fired?"

"What?" Danny says, distracted.

"I'm rehearsing the cannonball," Zamora says. "Remember? I'm not doing many more. Not sure it's the image I want to project for us dwarves . . ."

"I'll be there in a minute."

"You can press the trigger."

"Uh-huh."

The Major shrugs and stumps away to do the last checks on his equipment, leaving Danny and Sing Sing hunched over the pages of code.

"So what are they?"

"Dad's secrets. At first I thought they were just notes on his routines—the escapes and big prop tricks. But now I think these last few were related to his work for Interpol."

Laura has sent scans for three pages. On each of them is a chunk of code tucked between dated diary entries about the weather (*cold enough to freeze the tail off a brass monkey*), the quality of various shows (*Amsterdam—a shocker. Joey IMPOSSIBLE*), and seemingly mundane reports (*just got back from B and Full accounts by next week*). Here and there are a few indecipherable smudges where pencil has been hastily rubbed out.

Other surviving fragments betray more.

Lily not happy. But can sort it out after the 12th.

AKI knows! (Aki knows what? Why couldn't Dad be clearer?)

Snapped at Danny. Am letting him down a bit. That brings back another chunk of unwanted emotion, but he blocks it out, focuses on the codes.

The first, dated February 3rd, and all underlined, reads:

7270277172563 67367076720456
73472866 721 6776 6761677076
688668606l 853 876577 891272
668717 68668606l 60061606 472
62170 7061866!! CLUE: I am not
Houdini but the man himself.

The second, dated February 6th:

38669 08887 600l8 36838 99l82 88291
90958 03458 248989—81738 64629 09133
86482 490354! CLUE: All around us. All
the time. LATIN!

The last of them, the very last entry in the diary, scrawled urgently, and dated the day before the fire:

7.|.5| 9.5.|2 7.|.5 35.3.8 24.30.3 24.8.4
86.3|.3: |3.20.2 + |32.||.|! CLUE: This one
takes THE BISCUIT! Remember?

Sing Sing whistles. "I can't even do crosswords! What kind of code is it?"

"Looks like three different kinds. We used to do a lot of pigpen—you know, the one that looks like bits of a tic-tac-toe game?"

Sing Sing looks blank.

"They're easy to crack. Even when there's a keyword scrambling it up. Dad would always put a clue for that. Just like here. We used to do some others . . ."

Danny's been concentrating so hard he hasn't heard the Klowns drifting over, gathering around him, crouched now on the bench to either side. Bjorn's got his skull mask pulled down. Aki's smiling, his piercings glinting in the Mysterium lights. Joey's frowning at the pages in Danny's hands.

"What you got there, Daniel?" Joey says. Instinctively Danny pulls the pages tight to his chest.

"Looks like Harry's writing. Some kind of code too?" Aki says, his eyes boring into the paper clutched in Danny's hands.

"He liked his secrets," Bjorn says quietly, his voice blurred by the mask.

"Let me have a look," Aki says, forcing himself between Danny and Sing Sing on the bench.

"Watch it, fish face," Sing Sing snaps.

"I could help you," Aki says. "And I saw my name there."

"*I am not Houdini but the man himself,*" Joey reads, biting his lip, trying to get a better look. "Hmmm."

Danny gets to his feet. This is *way* too uncomfortable. The Klowns have always put him a bit on edge, even though they can be good fun at times. But with his suspicions running fast against them, with his growing belief that one of them may have harmed Dad, they seem now positively dangerous.

"It's nothing to do with you," he says, backing away. "And I've got to help Zamora."

He glances over to where the cannon has been placed on its taped marks. Zamora is standing by it, checking the trajectory, strapping his crash helmet on tightly. Frankie is there too, smoothing imaginary hair on his bald head, winding a long tape measure back into its holder.

"Don't be shy," Joey says. "We just want to help."

"Leave him be," Sing Sing snaps. "He said it's his business, now butt out!"

"And who do you think *you* are?" Joey fires back, his red hair twitching.

Danny turns and walks away toward Zamora and the cannon, eager to be away from the Klowns' prying eyes, but only to be overtaken by Aki.

"I'll race you, Danny. First one there fires Zamora!" he shouts. "And by the way, I think I know what one of those codes is."

There's a howl of pain from behind now. Danny looks back to see Joey rolling on the floor dramatically, clutching his stomach, while Sing Sing stalks away, shaking her head and muttering under her breath.

"What did you do that for?!"

"Not now," Zamora barks. "Cut it out, Klowns! I need to concentrate." He stomps back over toward the prone Joey, who continues to milk attention, rolling and groaning on the floor, leaving Danny marooned halfway between them and the cannon. He looks around.

Aki is hovering by the firing mechanism. There's the faint trace of a grin playing around the Japanese Klown's mouth. At what? Joey's terrible acting? The codes? Or, more innocently, how Herzog is frantically licking at Joey's face, trying to revive him?

"Come on, Danny," the Major says, returning to his equipment. "Forget that stupid Klown. And you, Aki—out of the way. I'm only trusting Danny to press the launch button." He looks meaningfully at the Klown, who simply shrugs his shoulders and slouches away into the shadows, muttering to himself.

"Knock yourself out! *Ganbatte kudasai.*"

Danny folds the coded pages neatly and slips them into his jeans pocket. Amidst all this uncertainty it's good to have Dad's messages tucked close to him.

Calm—or at least a semblance of it—returns to the cathedral nave. Billy picks up his guitar and starts the crescendoing buildup to Zamora's Captain Soyuz routine.

"Cue video," Rosa shouts, clapping her hands.

A scratchy film of a Russian rocket launch starts to flicker on a loop, black-and-white images across the pillars, the floor, Zamora.

Frankie and Bjorn move to either side of the distant catching net about a hundred feet away across the brooding cathedral, while Rosa plants herself at the halfway point, ready to trace Zamora's flight with a dramatically outstretched arm, as if following the trajectory of a shooting star.

The Major snaps into performance mode—and he's as good as ever—taking Danny's attention away from Aki and Joey, away from the codes for a second. He mimes fear, courage, determination as he climbs the ladder; crosses himself; and then slides, feet first, down the barrel. Danny's hand hovers over the red launch button. When he presses it the spring mechanism will release, firing the Major into the air, simultaneously detonating a whiz-bang that is fitted to the base of the gun. And Zamora will hurtle in a looping arc, one arm extended, all the way to the safety of the net.

This feels good, though, Danny thinks. *To be part of a rehearsal.* He looks around as the music builds. Aki and Joey are sitting on the stone bench now, leaning forward, watching with close attention.

The crackly Russian voice counts down, booming over the guitar. "*Tri . . . Dva . . . Udin . . .*"

Now!

Danny's hand plunges the red button down, and the detonation shakes through his palm.

At that precise moment, Javier bursts from the shadows. His face is creased with concern, mouth open, a hand reaching out. He's shouting, but his voice is lost against the fury of the guitar, the roar of the thunderclap.

The explosion has never sounded so loud—it hammers back off the stone walls and pillars as Zamora takes flight.

But immediately Danny sees the trajectory's wrong. Horribly wrong. The Major's arms are flapping—hopelessly trying to correct as he veers well to the left of the catching net. With a sickening crunch, he slams into one of the pillars and screams out in pain, before falling heavily to the floor. His helmet smacks the flagstones as he lands.

For a moment the only sound is the reverberation of the thunderclap effect.

And then Rosa and Sing Sing are rushing to help, with the others close behind. Frankie's face has drained of all color, and he's looking from the cannon to the net and back again.

No, Danny thinks. *Not Zamora.*

But even in his anguish, he's aware enough to look down, checking to see where the cannon rests on its taped crosses. Yes! It's been moved.

But only by a fraction. Not enough to make Zamora miss the net by that much—and it could just have been the force of the recoil. Danny looks around—and there in a doorway, for a brief second, sees a figure turn and take flight. A quick flash of green.

Without another thought he's off in pursuit.

The door is cut into a corner of the nave, and Danny bundles through it to find himself at the foot of a sharply twisting stairwell. There's no handrail, and looking up, he gets a dizzying sense of vertigo watching the tight screw of the stairs disappearing into darkness above.

There are footsteps—hurried, scuffed—echoing down toward him.

"Stop!" he shouts, his voice sounding small, lost in the staircase.

No answer, so he starts to climb as fast as he can, holding out his left hand for support on the smooth wall, twisting up and up, shoes gripping the smooth steps.

"Stop!" he shouts again. But now, filtering down the stairway, comes a burst of laughter. It's hysterical, slightly out of control—a high-pitched tumble, not a trace of joy in it, like someone trying to swallow back a torrent of nervous energy.

For a second he hesitates, the sound so chilling that his courage falters. What kind of a person laughs like that? Can't give up now, can't be afraid of the dark and a little bit of laughter—no matter how eerie. It's receding now, almost faded completely. Get a move on.

He attacks the stairs again, taking the steps two at a time, legs starting to work quickly into oxygen debt, his muscles burning. After five more twists of the spiral he comes to another doorway. It's open—and through it he finds himself on a balcony of the Sagrada, the city spread out in bright points of light against the black sea beyond. Immediately before him, glowing orange in the cathedral's spotlights, is a vast forest of scaffolding clamped to the soaring towers. A crane towers over everything.

Not a sound to be heard but the growl of the traffic below. No movement on the balcony or the scaffolding. He edges along the walkway to where it dives back in through another small door. Is that a shadow on a walkway higher above? Can't be sure.

The wind gusts, ruffling his hair as he strains to listen. And then, just audible, from somewhere far away, comes that laughter again. After a few seconds it cuts off abruptly. No way to tell whether it comes from above or below, from inside the building or out amid the three-dimensional labyrinth of the scaffold.

Danny takes a breath, listens to the wind whispering on the netting, but hears nothing more—and then he turns and hurries back down the stairs to his stricken friend.

Even as he crosses the cathedral toward the immobile form of Zamora, he's checking for clues, studying the floor near the cannon. Yes, the prop is definitely off its marks by a fraction—but a good pace or two away, just about visible, are the telltale traces of adhesive of another set of crosses. As if the gaffer tape has been placed once, then pulled up and stuck down again a short way off . . . He bends and touches the ghost marks and feels the glue still tacky there.

Then he hurries to Zamora.

———————————

Far out in the scaffolding La Loca is breathing as deeply as she can, doing her best to contain the burst of energy that has just pulsed through her body. Her black coat flaps in the breeze, revealing a flash of the green lining.

For once things aren't going entirely according to plan for her. Not absolutely perfect. How did the boy catch sight of her? It's put her in a bad mood, and that's why that stupid laughter has come rushing back at her. But tomorrow is another day, she tells herself, working to calm the rage building within—and it will find her back at the top of her game. She's sure of that. She can take out two birds with one stone if she plays it right. Maybe get a bonus! At least that stupid midget's out of action. No way could he stand that impact. Her so-called accomplice has actually exceeded expectations. Nicely done.

Rest in peace, Mister Dwarf.

The thought calms her more. Slowly, quietly, she starts to work her way down to the ground far, far below.

17

WHY DETAILS HIDE DEVILS

But Zamora is made of tougher stuff.

To Danny's relief he comes back to consciousness after five long minutes. His right arm is bent banana-like the wrong way, and there's a concussion from the blow to his head—but, even as he's being loaded into the back of an ambulance, he manages a smile, beckoning Danny over.

"Come with me, *amigo*?"

"Of course!" *That's good*, Danny thinks. He wants to be by his friend's side, and it will give him a moment alone with Zamora. *I need to tell him about the cannon marks—and I don't want anyone else listening.* That spooky laughter has unnerved him too, and he's eager to be away from the cathedral. At least for a bit.

The Major is looking past him now, searching the concerned faces of the assembled company. "Rosa. You too."

"Just try and stop me."

Blast. Not on our own, then! But Rosa needs to know too.

"What about me?" Sing Sing says, putting a foot onto the ambulance's step.

Danny shakes his head, whispering quickly in her ear. "Stay here. Keep your eyes and ears open and see what people are saying. Someone moved the cannon."

Sing Sing's eyes open wide—as if digesting the news or about to protest—but then she nods and hops back down. "Take care, Danny."

"You too," he says, realizing in that moment how glad he is to see her.

Javier's watching Zamora being loaded into the ambulance, his face white, then turns away, tears welling in his eyes. "I tried to warn him," he says. "Something looked wrong with the angle. I tried . . ."

The ambulance howls its way through the grid of streets toward the Hospital de Sant Pau.

Every now and then Zamora grimaces in pain, and for a while nobody has anything to say. Rosa shakes her head, trying to take in what has happened, while Danny wonders how to break the news. After all, he'll be making a direct accusation against a member of the company. He watches the ringmistress. By and large he trusts Rosa, but he still wonders what she was doing in the prop store on the night of the fire. Something about her actions that night felt wrong. As if some kind of guilt sharpened her movements as she tucked something away in a corner. And she's not going to be pleased to hear someone has deliberately injured Zamora. Will she even listen to the other stuff?

They bang over a pothole, and Zamora bites back a cry of discomfort that makes Danny wince in sympathy.

Rosa scowls. "Javier says the cannon was a teeny bit off the marks. He tried to warn you—"

"Wasn't enough to miss by that much," the Major says, gritting his teeth. "We must have set up wrong. Frankie checked the distance just before, and we did the alignment earlier. Fired the test dummy. Direct hit!"

"Just chalk it up to bad luck," Rosa says, crossing herself. "I knew my tarot cards were telling me something—"

"Unless," Danny says, "unless someone moved the tape."

"What?!" Rosa's eyebrows shoot up. "What are you talking about?"

"I think someone moved the gaffer tape. So when the cannon was wheeled back into place it was all wrong."

Rosa shakes her head vigorously.

"You can't be serious, Danny! Who would want to hurt Major Zee? Besides, you would have seen the angle was out, wouldn't you, Zamora?"

"Possibly." The Major grimaces again. "I was a bit preoccupied."

"But it's ridiculous—"

"We were distracted," Danny says, his voice gaining strength. "The Klowns were making a fuss. Just before."

"But I don't see—"

Zamora scowls. "Danny thinks the Klowns— one or more of them—might have been involved in Harry's accident in the water cell." He tries to sit up on the stretcher, but the paramedic stops him, trying to stabilize the broken arm.

Danny watches Rosa's reaction. She closes her mouth tight, as if she was about to say something and then thought better of it. She looks Danny in the eyes, that quick temper returning.

"Why do you say that, Danny?"

"Because I remember seeing that one of them had paint on his knee. The same paint that was wet on the equipment. They must have climbed up on top. Plugged the locks or something. I saw it when they came running to help."

"Nonsense."

"And the Klowns made the distraction just before the cannon . . ."

"Sing Sing said you chased someone up the tower. After the accident."

"I think it was a woman. She was laughing—but in a horrible way. It was weird . . ." His voice trails off. The pursuit is already starting to seem unreal, his head blurring from the stress of the day.

"Crazy places attract crazy people. The guards tell me all kinds of weirdos hang around the place. I'm more worried about what you're saying about the Klowns."

The ambulance is braking now, bumping up a ramp. Zamora pushes the paramedic to one side and sits up, his face deathly pale from the pain and shock but determined.

"It's worse than that, Rosa. I haven't had a chance to tell you, but it seems that Harry was involved in some . . . um . . . very dangerous business, away from the Mysterium. Danny and I suspect someone was responsible for Harry and Lily's death—"

"Not you too—"

The ambulance doors are swung open then. Danny and Rosa watch as the dwarf's stretcher is loaded onto a wheeled stretcher. Above them, burning against the night, the massive letters above the accident and emergency bay shine red, spelling out a single word: *URGENCIAS*.

Danny glances up at it, the light spilling across his face, his eyes. The ringmistress has to listen. "Please, Rosa. I think it's true."

She looks at him, biting her lip, coming to a decision. "We'll work on the assumption that we have to be careful and that there might be a tiny, *tiny* bit of truth in what you say, Danny. You and Sing Sing can sleep in my caravan. To be on the safe side. But I can't believe the worst of what you say. I won't."

Zamora winces again as his arm is bound into place on his chest. "Think about it, Rosa. Aki certainly had some links to the yakuza back in Tokyo. And Joey? Well, God only knows what he got up to in Montpellier!"

"Then we'll have formal circus disputation tomorrow morning," Rosa says decisively. "Clear the air. Ask them out straight."

That's better, Danny thinks. *But it's going to be pretty scary.*

The night presses down on the Sagrada.

Slowly, one by one, the company has digested the news that Zamora will need to have surgery—a pin put through the double fracture to his arm—and that he will be out of action for at least six weeks. A mixture of relief and bewilderment shows on their faces as they head to their accommodations in rented flats around the square. Danny is very wary around the Klowns, but their reactions seem genuine now, their concern heartfelt. Only at one point do alarm bells ring: when Aki sidles over, puts a strong grip on Danny's shoulder, and whispers, "If you need help with those codes, Danny, come to me first. I'm your man."

Danny glances at the chopped-off ring finger as Aki's hand releases its grip.

"I'm fine, thanks."

The Klown hesitates, then shrugs and slips away into the dark belly of the cathedral.

It's way past midnight by the time Danny and Sing Sing are tucked up on the bench seats on either side of Rosa's caravan table. Sing Sing is cocooned in a spare sleeping bag, her head pulled way down inside, just a few strands of her long dark hair spilling onto a pillow. Danny rolls himself in a couple of blankets, trying to get comfortable, trying to still his restless mind.

Outside he can just make out Rosa's silhouetted form, wrapped up in her big puffy coat, smoking her way through first one, then two, then three cigarettes. *She must be really stressed*, he thinks. She vowed she'd never smoke again, not after her father died so miserably of lung cancer—the great aerialist Paolo Vega "brought to earth at fifty-eight by a hundred thousand stupid cigarettes," as she always used to say.

And something else is bothering him now: before bed Rosa had fished out a bundle from her shoulder bag. A large deck of cards wrapped in blue silk.

"I need to do my tarot. See what's going on," she said, carefully unwrapping them.

Danny peered cautiously at the gaudy, antique cards. Always the deck had fascinated him—but scared him too: the images somehow familiar *and* strange, packed with ominous meaning. A horned devil presiding over two naked prisoners, a moon staring sternly down at a baying dog and wolf, a fool stepping over a cliff edge with a smile on his face . . . Dad said Rosa used the cards to give you advice, to tell you what you needed to do. *It's not that she predicts the future*, he would say, *but she can sort of think with them. See the forest for the trees, if you like.*

"Do them for me," Danny said on an impulse. "Would you?"

"You sure?"

"I was always too scared to ask. When I was little," he added.

Rosa smiled. "OK, Danny. OK. Let's see what they say."

She spread the cards facedown on the table, shuffling them, sliding their chevron backs across one another—the clashing patterns oddly hypnotic—and then gathered them back together again.

"We'll just do a quick-style reading. Then sleep. Ready?"

Danny nodded.

"This first card," Rosa said, picking the top one from the deck, "represents your past situation."

She flipped it over to reveal a startling image. A tall, lonely tower stood against the night sky, a lightning bolt splitting it asunder. Flames against black clouds. People spilling from battlements to the ground far below.

Rosa inclined her head.

"The Tower. Obvious in this position. Chaos, calamity. The end of something—no prizes for what we're talking about here: It's Berlin. We're in tune with the deck. So let's see what the next card has to say. That'll be the present, your current situation, Danny." He leaned forward. Curious. Cautious.

Flip. The second card landed next to the tower and revealed an even more bizarre image.

Rosa sucked her teeth. "The Hanged Man. Wow."

Danny peered at the card: a man suspended by one leg from a kind of gallows on a hill. But the gallows was made from living, leaf-sprouting wood, and—even more extraordinarily—the man was smiling calmly, his face lit by a glow of contentment as he dangled upside down. As if he knew something no one else knew.

"What does it mean?" Danny asked softly.

"The Hanged Man is suspended in time," Rosa said. "He's waiting for a moment of change. A decisive moment. It's beautiful, no? The Hanged Man is about seeing a situation clearly and then acting at just the right moment."

"What about the third one, then?"

"This is your future, Danny."

A premonition in that moment: *It's going to be something bad*, he thought. But Rosa was already snapping the third card into place.

Death. The death card. Danny remembered it in a flash—how it used to scare him when he flicked through Rosa's deck. A black skeleton in a suit of armor riding a white horse across a battlefield strewn with body parts, the dead, the dying. A chill flooded Danny's body.

"Now you know that doesn't mean death, don't

you?" Rosa said, hastily gathering the cards. "It can mean all manner of things."

"So what does it mean for me?"

"Just that we're in a bit of a pickle. That things might get a bit worse before they get better. It'll be fine in the end . . ." Her voice trailed off and she flashed him a smile, but for the rest of the evening she was silent, wrapped up in her own thoughts. Clearly spooked.

Now there's no chance of getting to sleep. The image of that skeleton on his white horse . . . *Wish I hadn't asked for the reading*, Danny thinks.

"Sing Sing?" he whispers.

Not a sound from the sleeping bag.

"Sing Sing!"

"What?"

"Are you awake?"

"I am now," she says peevishly, her voice muffled.

"What are you doing here?"

"Auditioning."

"Apart from that. What are you really doing?"

There's a long silence.

"Sing Sing?"

He begins to wonder if she's gone back to sleep, but then, her voice suddenly clear as she pushes her head from the bag, she sighs. "If you must know, I'm looking for my mother."

"But you said she was dead."

"Life's very complicated sometimes."

"I don't understand."

"Neither do I." She sits up, her oval face lit by the moonlight spilling around the shoulder of the Sagrada. "Neither do I," she repeats, "but I do know one thing. I'm glad to see you."

She extends a hand across the table—and Danny reaches out to take it for a moment.

"Me too," he says, and the touch feels at once familiar, comforting. "Whatever happens, let's stick together?"

"You bet," she says. "Now get some sleep, dummy."

"*Wan an.*"

"That's Mandarin," Sing Sing says. "I thought your mum was a Hong Konger. Didn't she speak Cantonese to you?"

"Does it matter?" he sighs, a bit annoyed at being corrected.

"Maybe," Sing Sing says. "The devil's in the flipping details."

When Danny's eyes eventually do close, he sinks into a world stalked by skeletons and red-faced, laughing demons.

18

WHY JIMMY GOT THE BOOT

A cloud-packed morning breaks across the city.

Danny stumbles to wakefulness, shaking the disturbed dreams from his head. It takes a full two minutes to work out where he is. Lying on his back on the caravan bench, he has the disorientating feeling that he's back in the family trailer—that familiar sense of a shared sleeping space, the sound of people breathing deeply near you, the slight rock of the thing as you move. He parts the orange curtains over his head and sees the towering form of the Sagrada, the lazy movement of one of the enormous cranes. That block of stone.

Then he remembers what's coming. Disputation with the Klowns. Confrontation. He takes a deep breath, lets it out slowly.

Rosa is already up and moving around at the other end of the caravan, sucking honey from a knife that she's just gouged into a jar.

"Danny! Sing Sing! Let's get to it. Day's wasting and I've got some Klowns to talk to—and a sore throat to boot."

"Urgh," Sing Sing groans from inside her bag. "I need more flipping sleep."

"If you're going to join us," the ringmistress mutters, "then you'd better get used to early starts, young lady." Again, that twinge of jealousy hits Danny. I *should be the one auditioning*, he thinks. *But doing what? Maybe I was just lucky to fight my way out of that freezer. Still, I wish Zamora had told them all about it.*

On the way back into the cathedral they meet Darko. He at least looks fresh, a towel draped around his neck after an early morning run.

"Rosa, I need a quick word."

"Can it wait? We've got to have this breakfast meeting. Figure out how we're going to fill in for Zamora. And one or two other things."

"Oh, really?" Darko glances at Danny, then Sing Sing, his quicksilver eyes bright with interest. "What haven't I been told?"

"We've got trouble," Rosa says. "We're pretty sure someone moved Zamora's cannon before the accident."

Danny winces slightly, wanting to keep the information closely guarded until they confront the Klowns.

"Are you OK, Danny?" Darko says, spotting his reaction.

"I'm just worried about Zamora."

"I'm going to question the Klowns after breakfast," Rosa says.

"I want to be there," Danny says urgently. "Or try to read them without them knowing."

"In case you're forgetting," Rosa snaps, "I'm the director of this show. It's great having you here, Danny, but you're a guest. Nothing more. I make the decisions."

That stops Danny short—like a jab to the stomach, taking the wind from him. Just a guest. And tomorrow or the day after or next week, he'll be gone, and they'll carry on without him. That's almost as hard to deal with as the fact that someone's out to hurt him, he realizes. It matters that much!

Rosa hasn't finished.

"And Danny and the Major have this crazy

notion that the same person sabotaged the water torture cell. But why would anyone have wanted to hurt Harry?"

"Well, if I was looking for someone to fit that bill," Darko says, carefully picking out each syllable, "I'd suggest Jimmy T."

"Who's Jimmy T?" Sing Sing asks.

"Disgraced former member of the company," Darko says, turning back. "Danny's papa had to fire him. No choice."

Half a memory now: raised voices, slammed doors. Rosa's looking decidedly on edge again, Danny spots. She puts her hand through her hair. "Come on, Darko, he's a bit messed up, but—"

"I know you liked the man," Darko says, "but think about it."

"Why did your dad fire him?" Sing Sing asks, turning to Danny.

"His acts kept going wrong, and he put Izzy in danger one day—"

"No," Darko says. "It was worse than that, Danny."

"Not now—" Rosa throws her hands up in dismay.

"He might as well know," Darko says, looking at Danny.

"Know what?"

Here it comes, Danny thinks, *here comes another slice of the past that I don't think I want to hear. And yet at the same time I want to know. Need to know.*

"Darko?"

"He had become obsessed with your mum, Danny. Totally besotted. He kept pestering her and pestering her and she told him to back off, but he couldn't help himself. He was always in her face, too close, saying too much. In the end Harry told him to clear out. Jimmy went—but he didn't go willingly. Took a bit of *persuasion.* Your dad had a lot on his mind, I think, and he lost his temper and kicked him out. Literally."

Another secret. And not a nice one. Danny closes his eyes, feeling uncomfortable.

Rosa, fierce now, puts a finger to her lips. "Can't you see the boy's dealing with enough?"

"He might need to know. I mean, if someone's up to mischief? That kind of thing can make people very angry. Irrational."

"But it doesn't help," Danny says, recovering his balance a bit. "That may all be true—but Jimmy T. couldn't have been involved, could he? He was in the States when the accident—when both accidents—happened."

"That's true," Rosa says, nodding. "He was doing the run in that Oblivion show. And he can't be involved with this business last night."

"In which case," Darko says, "you'd better have your chat with the Klowns. And maybe Frankie too. He measured the thing out, after all."

They all head inside, but Danny hangs back for a moment. The early morning traffic pulses around the cathedral. Dust and litter swirl in the stiffening breeze. *Dad was always going on about mystery,* he thinks, *how vital it was to make you feel alive.* But maybe that was all just bluff, covering for things he didn't want people to know. The man Danny knew and the one that's emerging seem like different men. This new one had a whole other life, bad arguments with other members of the troupe, grudges held against him. This whole business of Mum and Jimmy T., and Dad chucking Jimmy out! He was still Dad, though, wasn't he?

Danny shoves his hands in his pockets—feels the smooth metal of the carabiner lurking there—and, crackling next to it, the pages of code.

Almost forgot about them, he thinks, looking up, his mood lifting just that little bit. Beyond the brooding towers, the clouds are thinning, breaking up, their ragged edges glowing as sunlight starts to burn its way through.

But breakfast is a somber affair. The company members look bleary-eyed and downcast as they assemble around the trestle table. Danny glances from one to the other, but it seems no one but Sing Sing will meet his gaze for long. It's as if they're all keeping him at arm's length, reluctant to acknowledge his presence. Why? Guilt, maybe? Or more secrets still to come?

Sing Sing smiles reassuringly, though, and that helps calm his nerves. Rosa seems to think that she will confront the Klowns and everything will come out just fine and peachy. But he's worried about how Aki, Joey, and Bjorn will react. As Zamora once said, they gave you the willies at the best of times. What will happen when they're cornered?

"What about my audition, Rosa?" Sing Sing chirps.

"We'll see about that later, *bella*," Rosa says. "Got

enough on my plate right now. You need to stay put and keep out of harm's way."

Her gaze swivels to the Klowns, who are sitting in a tight knot at the foot of the table. *Here it comes*, Danny thinks and braces himself.

"I want a full run-through this morning. But first, I want to see Aki, Joey, and Bjorn in the prop store. Circus disputation."

The Klowns look up in unison, surprised.

"Disputation? Why?" Bjorn growls.

"Because I said so," Rosa snaps. "We need to clear the air."

Joey rolls his eyes, his red hair floppy, disheveled. "Is that an order, Madame Vega?"

Aki gazes down into his cup of coffee and pulls a face. "If you've got something to say, say it now. Let's not waste time with that disputation crap."

"That's how we always do things," Rosa says. "Open, honest. And Danny's going to sit in on the conversation. Then we can all be friends again, can't we?"

That's good, he thinks, his heartbeat quickening. *At least I'll have a chance to watch their reactions, see how Rosa's questions strike them—even if it will all be a bit confrontational. Scary.*

He glances out through the window into the courtyard. A shadow passes—the long boom arm of one of the cranes briefly blocking the light.

Ten minutes later, Danny and Rosa are sitting on flight cases in the prop store, waiting for the first of the Klowns.

The back of the trailer is still half full of equipment and costumes from older shows, acts that don't feature in the revived show: a gleaming German wheel, spare trapeze rigging, fire hoops, the chainsaws for the Klowns, a drum marked STAGE BLOOD. Hanging on a wall is Dad's old white straightjacket. *Man, that thing used to give me the creeps*, Danny thinks. *I always hated seeing him fastened into it like someone in a Victorian asylum. Never minded the cuffs and chains, but that thing . . .*

He shivers, pulls his eyes away, and turns to watch the ringmistress closely. She looks commanding, but the toe of her right boot is tapping the floor in quick time. Hardly noticeable, but it's enough to show that beneath the cool, collected surface she's kicking like crazy.

"Remember the point of circus disputation," she says rapidly. "We're not trying to have an argument. We're trying to find common ground. What we agree on. Let me do the talking."

"Ask them about the paint. And about Zamora's cannon marks."

"Let's just tread carefully before we throw too much mud around, OK?"

Rosa takes a breath and shouts to Darko, who's waiting outside. "OK!" She lifts her chin, as if about to face an opponent in the boxing ring. "Let's have Bjorn." Danny tenses, hands gripping the seat, feeling suddenly exposed. *But I'm ready*, he thinks. *I'll let Rosa do most of it and watch the reactions, watch for giveaways as they answer.*

The catcher steps into the trailer and stands, solid, impassive, blocking out the light.

"Bjorn. Have a seat," Rosa says quietly.

The big man flashes Danny a smile. It's hard to read and is gone in a moment, but it wasn't a friendly greeting. Could have been defensive? Maybe even masked aggression? Those could look the same. Danny remembers again that evening when, without warning of any kind, Bjorn had punched his fist straight through the plywood wall.

"What's up, Rosa?"

"We need to clear the air—"

"Does it need clearing?"

"Apparently. Danny here has some concerns. I'll put them to you, and you tell us what you agree with. OK?"

Bjorn swivels to look at Danny. Holds his eyes for a beat. "Go. On."

"To be blunt, he wonders if you messed with Harry's water torture equipment, that night before the accident. Or maybe one of the others."

Bjorn's head whips back to look at Rosa. *She's struck some kind of nerve*, Danny thinks, *that much is for sure, but is it more than just anger?* He grips the box seat tighter, waiting. There's silence for a moment—and then Bjorn surges to his feet.

"WHAT? ME?!"

"Calm down. I'm asking everyone, sorting out this nonsense," Rosa says.

Bjorn turns to Danny, hands flexing, his habitual movement when about to catch a flyer—or hit something.

"You shouldn't chuck wild accusations about, Danny. This job is built on trust. If we don't trust each other, then how can we work? How can we let go of the bar and *fly*?"

Bracing himself, Danny decides he needs to speak. "But what about Zamora? Did you see anything—"

"No! And you should be careful about stirring things up. Some of the others are thinking maybe you're bad luck. You show up and everything starts to go wrong again . . ."

Danny flinches at the thought. Maybe that's why people were avoiding his gaze this morning. Only place more superstitious than a boat is under a big top, Zamora always says. *Or maybe it's true—maybe bad stuff is following me.*

"So you deny it?" Rosa says.

"Cross my heart. And hope to die."

"And you don't know anything else?" Rosa insists.

"You didn't see anyone else messing with the water tank?"

"Nothing. Nada. Zippo," the catcher says heavily, shaking his head vigorously. "And I've got better things to be doing than listen to this."

There's silence for a moment, and then Bjorn stamps across the floor of the trailer and is gone, leaving the vehicle rocking on its springs.

The ringmistress is rubbing her forehead with her palm. "Look, *bello*, perhaps better to leave this up to me . . .?"

"No. I'm staying," Danny says, trying to make his voice sound calm—at least calmer than he feels. "It's my business too."

"You're as stubborn as your papa." She looks him in the eyes. "He never knew when to let things drop. That can be a strength and a fault too, you know . . ."

Aki's already in the doorway, his expression bright, open. "Rosa-*san*. We all have our faults, right?"

His mood seems more upbeat than Bjorn's. Curious as to what's going on, rather than defensive, Danny thinks. That guarded look of yesterday is gone. *But what about how he reacted when I turned up after the chase on Las Ramblas?* Aki turns to look at him expectantly.

"Is it about your codes, Danny-*chan*?"

"No," Rosa says. "We've got important business to—"

"Because I reckon I know what the first one is," the Klown interrupts. "Remember how I used to help you with difficult ones, Danny? Looks like rail fence to me. You know, three rows. Numbers along the top with two missing . . .?"

"Aki!" Rosa says, impatiently. "Focus. I need to ask you something. I'm asking everyone."

"Everyone?" Aki snipes, his mood changing direction in a heartbeat. "Seems it's just us Klowns, to me. It's always us when there's trouble. Why don't you talk to the others too? This is about Zamora's accident, I guess, so why not talk to Frankie? He does the measurements."

He looks genuinely affronted, gripped tight with indignation. He massages the stumpy end of his shortened ring finger.

"Aki," Danny says, "you were near the cannon, that's all. Did you see anything last night? Anything odd?"

"You're asking if I gave it a push. Don't be stupid. Why would I do that? Why would *anyone* do that?"

"Because Danny thinks someone has been trying to hurt members of the company," the ringmistress says. "First, Harry. Now Zamora. You're sure you know nothing about that or the sabotage of the water cell?"

"No more than you do, Rosa," Aki says, shaking

his head hard, the black Mohawk vibrating. He gets to his feet, turning for the door. *Can't let him go without asking directly*, Danny thinks. *Need to be brave. Act it at least!*

"Someone plugged the locks on the water cell," he says, pitching his voice at Aki's back, "and I think it was one of you!"

The Klown stops then, framed in the doorway against the brighter light beyond.

"You're a clever boy, Danny. Like your dad and your mum. But you're wrong about this. And I'm a friend. *Tomodachi da yo!* Get it?"

He bangs the door frame with his fist on the way out, very hard. It makes Danny jump on his seat.

"Ignore him, Danny. He's just a grumpy old fool."

Danny looks at Rosa. She seems to have tensed her shoulders a bit more, and—while that's understandable, given Aki's temper—it feels like there's something else there now.

Weird what Aki said. "No more than you." That could mean "I know nothing" or "You and I know the same amount." Add that to the memory of the odd way Rosa behaved right here in the prop store on that snowy night in Berlin . . . maybe there's reason to suspect Rosa too? *Better tread very carefully,* he thinks.

"Ding-ding," Rosa says, looking distinctly uncomfortable. "End of round two. Let's see what Joey has to say. He's the toughest nut of the three."

19

WHY CLOWNING IS A SERIOUS BUSINESS

The Frenchman plops down on a rolled crash mat and turns an inquisitive face to Danny. He's wearing a sleeveless T-shirt, and Danny's eyes are drawn, as ever, to the puckered and blotchy scar tissue on his powerful arms. What horrific event must have put it there?

"Hey, Monsieur Danny. Is there a problem? My colleagues seem upset."

"Danny has some questions," Rosa says. "Can he ask them himself? I don't seem to be getting anywhere."

"Go on, Danny." Joey's eyes flash. "Ask me anything."

Danny isn't expecting that, not ready to be put on

the spot, and he takes a moment to steady his breathing, reach for the right words. The other two are staring at him and he feels small, alone. *If Zamora were beside me . . . or Sing Sing . . .* His eyes rove the wall of the trailer, glancing across Dad's old props, the coiled ropes, the straightjacket. The memory of Dad wriggling triumphantly free from the horrible thing—the relief and cheers that spread through the audience—gives him the extra bit of strength he needs.

"OK." Danny locks eyes with the Klown, holding his gaze, steadying himself. *You're meant to be honest in a disputation—so let's be honest.* "Did any of you fiddle with Dad's equipment? The night of the water cell accident?"

No response from Joey. His face as blank as one of the Klowns' masks.

"I mean, it might have been a prank that went wrong," Danny continues, more hesitantly. Still nothing. *So what do I do? Just keep going? Guess that's what Dad would do—stubborn.*

"Did you move the cannon marks . . . or get me chased on Las Ramblas yesterday . . .?"

Joey's eyes are opening wider now—as are Rosa's. Danny presses on, his heartbeat ramping up as he voices the pent-up suspicions.

"Or do you know why someone tried to drown me?"

Joey's holding up both hands, as if to stop the flow of words, his face now genuinely baffled. "Danny! What are you on about now?"

"Drown *you?*" Rosa echoes, puzzled. "Let's keep to the water cell, why don't we? And Zamora."

"I'm sure someone rigged the water cell," Danny says. He can't meet Joey's eyes now and looks away. "And that person was wearing a Klown skull mask."

"Then," Joey says, his voice spiked, "even *if* that's true, all you know for sure is that someone in a skull mask did it. And that could be anyone."

"But I saw everyone else." Danny glances back, trying to judge the Klown's reaction.

Joey looks away, rubbing the scar tissue on his left arm absentmindedly, trying to get hold of his temper.

Rosa is staring at the floor, holding her breath, her lips sealed tight. Isn't that a tell? A sign of feeling guilty about something?

Joey turns back, but the anger has gone and now it's replaced by something like disappointment. "What I'd like is a little respect around here. People should respect us clowns. People think it's all pratfalls and exploding cars, but we're so much more than that. We're the tricksters, Danny—sacred tricksters—and we have existed in all cultures, all times. And yes—if we're doing it right—we're here to make people laugh, but we're also here to make them feel on edge, uncomfortable. Like things are upside down. We're *supposed* to feel dangerous."

Joey looks directly at him. Their eyes lock for a second, and Danny does his best to hold the Klown's gaze.

"Please, Joey. If you know anything . . ."

Joey hesitates. "You might want to ask Aki something. I—I saw him talking to someone, a couple of days before your dad's accident. I don't want to tell tales, but . . ."

Come on, Danny thinks, *tell me what you know, then.* He leans back, trying to give Joey space now.

"Well, I saw Aki at the edge of the camp. He was talking to someone and it was dark and I couldn't see very well, but—"

"But you recognized him, didn't you?" Danny asks excitedly.

"*Oui.* I think it was Jimmy T."

"But it couldn't be," Rosa shouts, very abruptly. "Don't be stupid, Joey."

The Klown looks at Danny and shrugs. "I think it *was* him," Joey insists, matter-of-factly. He jumps to his feet. "But I don't know what he was doing here. And that's all I know. And now I'm off."

Bull's-eye, Danny thinks, his heart racing. *A new piece of the puzzle. And I got it out of him.* Even if he has no idea where that piece goes, Joey's testimony feels honest, direct.

He turns to Rosa. But her face is dark, stormy as she rummages fiercely in her bag. "Waste of time," she mutters. "I need to look at my cards again. Maybe they'll tell me something more useful. Maybe we have got some bad luck hanging over us."

The image of the death card flashes in Danny's mind. Maybe now's the time to confront the ring-mistress, while his courage and spirits are still up, while he has her to himself. I *need to know who I can count on—and who's still a question mark, a danger,* he thinks.

"Rosa," he says quietly. "Can I ask *you* a question about Jimmy?"

"No! You CANNOT!" Rosa snaps. "Haven't got time!"

She slings her bag over her shoulder, throws him a look of irritation, and bowls out through the door.

Danny slumps back on his seat.

There it is again. Rosa was all kindness when he turned up—treating him like a favorite nephew, just like she used to—until the subject turned to the sabotage of the cell. Now she's defensive, prickly. Even more so when Jimmy's name comes up. She likes Danny, he's sure, but she wishes he wasn't here. And she wishes the whole thing about Mum and Dad would just go away. But why?

He lets his breath go and looks up at Dad's old props again, the cuffs and shackles, the coiled rope. How much energy he spent escaping from those things over and over again. And for what?

A gust of wind buffets the trailer, rocking it on its springs. Then another. The suspension creaks—and it feels in that moment as if he's cast adrift on a wild and rolling sea.

20

WHY DEATH ISN'T ALWAYS THE END

Sing Sing is waiting impatiently in the performance space, chatting to Izzy and Beatrice, but as soon as she sees Danny, she runs over, her eyebrows raised.

"I got something out of Joey," Danny whispers. "He says Jimmy Torrini might have been hanging around before my dad's accident."

Sing Sing whistles softly. "And after what Blanco said about him! Maybe he messed with the locks to get revenge."

"But we were all sure he was in New York then. It doesn't make sense. And now Rosa's cross with me. And the other two . . ."

Danny looks around. There's no sign of the ringmistress, but Javier is coming toward them. He looks tired, his strong face rumpled from lack of sleep—or bad dreams of his own.

"Hey," he says flatly. "I just called the hospital. Zamora's in surgery, but he should be out by late afternoon. Want to come with me to get him?"

"Yes, please," Danny says. It'll be good to see the Major—and perhaps *he* will be able to make sense of the new information.

"I'll meet you here at five. I've got some problems up at my club on Montjuïc to sort out first," Javier says miserably. "Sit tight until then, right? Don't go anywhere. We can't be too careful after yesterday."

"Don't worry," Danny says, trying to make his response sound as convincing as possible. "We're not going anywhere."

"Good," Javier says, forcing a smile. There's that same look of fear there, the one that passed between him and Lope in the doorway to their apartment. The kind of look when you think the ground might just give way beneath your feet.

"Good," Javier says again and turns away with a heavy roll of his shoulders.

They watch him go, his tall figure quickly lost in the vast and busy space of the cathedral.

"So?" Sing Sing says. "Are you going to tell me

what else happened in the disputation?"

"Later. Right now we're off to do some proper detective work."

"Rosa told us to stay put. And Javier."

"Since when did you start doing what you were told?" It's funny to be feeling bolder than his new friend for once. "And right now I don't really care what Rosa says."

He heads toward the main doors, his stride lengthening, and Sing Sing hurries after him.

"But where are we going?"

"To find out how we get to Tibidabo, of course."

Crossing the square to the metro, Danny's mind is hard at work.

The sheets of scanned code are rustling in his pocket, nestled next to the carabiner. Maybe Aki really was trying to be helpful. But then, if he's clean, why didn't he mention that whole thing about Jimmy? Maybe Joey's lying . . .

Well, we can have a look at the code on the way up to Tibidabo, he thinks. *I can just about remember how to do rail fence.*

"Oi, Danny," Sing Sing says, leapfrogging a traffic post. "I'm here, remember?"

"Sorry."

"Why are we going to this silly old fairground then?"

"That's where the body was found. The one with the forty-nine dots burned onto it. It must have been put there for a reason. He was either killed there or dumped there deliberately. We need to find out why."

"OK. I'm with you every step. But I hope Rosa doesn't end up mad at me. I want her to give my audition a fair viewing."

"I'll tell her it's my fault. You'll be fine," Danny says, his curiosity about Sing Sing's act tweaked again. "I want her to see my act too," he says quickly.

"Doesn't she know about the escape?" Sing Sing says. "That's the most amazing thing I've ever seen. And I didn't even get to actually see it!"

Danny smiles, glad of the recognition, warmed by Sing Sing's praise. *At least she knows what I can do!* "Haven't told her yet," he says. "And besides, I'll have to get a proper act together first."

The sun has broken through now, and green parakeets go screeching loudly overhead, stitching patterns between the trees. Crowds are already clustering around the cathedral, drawn by its power, like iron filings pulled to a magnet. *Need to keep our guard up*, he thinks and glances around, eyes searching for a figure that doesn't fit, for a person who seems more intent on them than the crazy towers of the Sagrada.

A gaggle of schoolchildren. A couple of young men strolling behind them, wrestling with a tourist map, heading toward the metro, arguing about directions. There's a group of traders, like the ones on Las Ramblas, setting out their wares on blankets. Whatever language they're speaking to one another, it's not Spanish or Catalan. Quick fingers, even quicker eyes—all tuned for the first glimpse of the police.

Sing Sing looks at them thoughtfully. "Hard to be an immigrant," she says, "when you have to fight to get your feet in a new place." Something in the way she says the words carries the conviction of personal experience, emotion in her voice.

"Has that happened to you?"

"To my mum," Sing Sing answers, smiling at one of the men who's holding out a bracelet. "She had to grow up very fast. Learn a new language, Cantonese.

Adapt and do her best . . ." Her words stutter to a halt and she pulls a face.

"Last night you said you were looking for her," Danny says, "but I don't understand. You said she was dead."

"There's dead—and then there's dead," Sing Sing says, hurrying on. "You know what I mean?"

"Not really."

"Chinese concept called *Hu*," she says, rapid-fire. "Ancestral soul. There's physical self, intelligence, spirit, emotional self—and then there's an ancestral self. It lasts three generations—as long as people can remember the things you did and said, as long as your life still affects other people's. The Hu can be alive long after the rest is dead. Makes sense, right?" she adds brightly. "So that's how you can be alive and dead at the same time. Maybe a bit of my mum's still here. Come on, let's look at your code on the subway." And with that she grabs hold of the handrail of the metro steps and leaps down the first flight in one long vault.

Danny hurries down the steps after her. He's so preoccupied that he doesn't see the two scruffy young men behind them look up from their map and hastily fold it, before quickening their own steps to follow.

Sitting side by side on the metro, Danny and Sing Sing stare at the paper in front of them. The movement of the train bumps their shoulders against each other, and the physical contact feels good—supportive and familiar somehow. Danny sneaks a look at Sing Sing's profile reflected in the window. *I like her*, he thinks. *I like her a lot. Feels more than just a friendship somehow . . .*

He remembers Zamora teasing him about Sing Sing being a girlfriend and feels warmth come to his cheeks again. Girlfriend? Too confusing. Doesn't feel right either.

"You OK, Danny?"

"Yep. Just trying to work this out." He flattens out the paper on his knee with quick movements of his hand. "We need to crack the keyword," he says, shoving the other thoughts away.

Sing Sing peers at it again. "*I am not Houdini, but the man himself.* It sounds weird. I know who Houdini was, of course—but how can you *not* be him, but *be* him at the same time?"

"Dad was obsessed with him. Not just the escapes but his whole life story, who he was, how he kept reinventing himself. Must be something to do with that."

"Like what?"

Danny closes his eyes, repeating the information like a well-learned school lesson. "Born 1874 in Budapest. Real name Erich Weiss. The family moved to the States when he was four, and he learned English fast. He started to work with his brother, doing tricks, picking locks, rope walking. He had various show names—Prince of the Air, King of Cards—but then he settled on Houdini. He thought it was French for 'like Houdin,' but it wasn't!"

"Who was Houdin?"

"Legendary magician. He kind of invented the whole of modern magic . . ."

His voice dies away. That's it, of course! He slaps the paper triumphantly with the back of his hand.

"Houdin—not Houdini. The man himself."

"He's hidden it in the open," Sing Sing says admiringly. "Now that's clever."

It feels really good to hear someone praising Dad after all the negative stuff Danny's been hearing recently. "He had his faults for sure—far more faults than I knew, in fact—but he wasn't stupid. And who knows how hard it was to balance directing the

Mysterium with the stuff he was doing for Interpol."
And there was me nagging away to play at codes, to learn new tricks! Like a little kid!

The train's pulling into the terminus, laboring up a long slope, and the few remaining passengers are getting to their feet.

Sing Sing smiles. As if reading his mind, she puts a hand on his shoulder. "Don't blame yourself, Danny. That's always a bad idea. Take it from me!"

As Danny and Sing Sing shuffle toward the barrier, the two men in gray hoodies edge closer. One of them reaches for a phone and thumbs a number on the screen. The other pulls his hood up, his eyes tight on Danny's and Sing Sing's backs, and works quickly through the crowd, closing the gap, until he's right behind them.

21

WHY A LOWLIFE CAN BE EASY TO SPOT

Near the metro exit, at the bottom of a steep ramp of a street, an old-fashioned tram waits to take them up out of the city. It's painted an intense sky blue, and its color and the parting clouds overhead seem to match Danny's lifting mood. *We're on our way to investigate a murder scene,* he thinks. *Zamora's in the hospital—and I'm in real danger. So why do I feel so much more hopeful? Better than I have for days, in fact?*

He glances at his companion. Of course, cracking the keyword feels like another important step forward. But Sing Sing's presence must have more than a bit to do with it. It feels like she's appeared—reappeared—in his life at just the right moment. As if it was scripted. Somehow her secrecy and evasions seems easier to deal with than Zamora's.

As they clamber aboard, squeezing together onto a wooden bench seat, Danny's reminded of riding the tram in Hong Kong.

He smiles at Sing Sing. "At least now I know you," he says. "Or trust you, anyway!"

"What?"

"Last time we were on something like this, Zamora and I were following you. We thought you were a triad yourself."

"And I saw you two dummies at once. As if you two could blend in!" Sing Sing snorts. "But I'm glad you trust me now."

A bell rings. A jolt of electricity puts life into the tram and it pulls away, grinding up the hill between expensive houses, an exclusive-looking school, a hospital, the space between the buildings allowing the wealth here to breathe.

"Come on then," Sing Sing says eagerly. "How does this rail fence thing work?"

"Well, you make a kind of grid." Danny turns the paper over. He takes out a pen and starts to scribble. "You put the numbers zero to nine across the top like this, and then you have two numbers at the side."

"But which?"

"You skip two when you put the keyword letters along the top row. And those two become the numbers at the side."

"How do you know which to skip?"

"That's the tricky bit. But there's a clue here. He's put an ampersand"—he points to the *&*—"and then three numbers on their own. So they've got to be single numbers for *A*, *N* and *D*, haven't they? Eight, five and three." Danny's pen is working fast now and forming the grid.

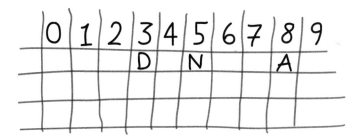

"Yes!" Sing Sing jabs the paper. "So you can put in your keyword, right? Houdin? It fits!"

"Then the rest follow alphabetically. You carry on after *A* and leave out the letters in HOUDIN. Which means six and seven go at the side." Danny bends over the paper, absorbed in his task, fiddling the letters into their places.

0	1	2	3	4	5	6	7	8	9
H	O	U	D	I	N			A	B
6 C	E	F	G	J	K	L	M	P	Q
7 R	S	T	V	W	X	Y	Z		

He leans back in triumph, eyes bright. "See? Now we can read off the numbers. If it's a six or seven, then it's a double digit. So 67 is *M*, for example. Seventy-one is *S*."

But Sing Sing's attention has slipped from what he's saying. She digs Danny gently in the ribs with her elbow, slipping the words quietly from the corner of her mouth.

"When we get off here, we're going to run like the devil."

"Why?"

"Because there're a couple of lowlife types following us."

"Are you sure?"

"Pretty sure."

"How do you know they're lowlifes?"

"Believe me, Danny. I've met enough."

The tram is rumbling around a long right-hand

bend, wheels squealing on the rail, pulling up toward the top station. Already Barcelona is spread wide below them, the regular grid of the modern city giving way to the twisted streets of the old quarter.

"Two idiots in hoodies. Bottom-feeders. Don't look round."

"So let's go!" Danny whispers. Even before the tram has slowed he's leapt to his feet, pushing through the other passengers. Sing Sing follows close behind, past the conductor who is motioning them to wait, and together they jump to the pavement from the moving carriage, hitting the ground hard and running.

The little square is almost empty. Above them the hillside is thickly wooded, and Danny can make out a cable railway pulling up through the trees toward the top. There's no obvious path, though. He looks back. The two hoodies are off the tram now, but they don't know whether to give chase or still pretend to be innocent tourists. That indecision gives Danny and Sing Sing the time they need. A solitary taxi is just about to pull away from the funicular station, but Danny's quickly across the ground and thumping on the window.

"Tibidabo, *por favor*." The driver nods.

They slide onto the backseat, and as they pull away, Danny turns to scout the parking lot behind them. The two men stand arguing in the deserted square—one of them putting a phone up to his ear, the other looking around desperately for another taxi.

"We've got a head start at least. They'll have to walk or wait for the cable car," Danny says.

"Losers," Sing Sing spits, shaking her head. "Charlie wouldn't have recruited them. Just have to hope they haven't got friends up ahead."

Danny leans forward to the driver, fishing for the right words. "Quickly, please. Um . . . *rapide?*"

"*Si. Rapidament.*"

The driver smiles and then stomps down on the accelerator, pushing past spandex-clad cyclists, up toward the brow of the hill, the exhaust from his yellow-and-black cab smudging on the breeze.

By now it's a gorgeous autumn day up at Tibidabo.

The woman in the lime-green coat hands her ticket stub to the attendant and looks out at the wide sweep of the city below. *It feels good to revisit the scene of a crime*, she thinks. *The police always expect you to do*

*that, of course—but they never spot me. Because nobody
saw me in the first place.*

She waits amid the excitable children and their
fussing mothers, watching the two-tiered merry-
go-round slow to a stop, the sunlight catching the
painted horses with their flared nostrils, the mirrors
behind them reflecting the rest of the fairground.

When it's her turn she pushes past a couple of
arguing kids and climbs to the top tier, where she
mounts a black stallion. A small girl tugs at the hem
of her coat, asking if she can have the horse, but the
woman just shakes her head and looks away across
the rest of Tibidabo.

"It's mine."

When the girl's mother sees what has happened,
she comes striding up the steps, throwing a stream of
angry Spanish at the woman.

One turn of the head, one hissed word that
nobody else catches, and the mother backs off,
mouth open in shock, and leads her child away with
a backward glance at the woman astride *her* fairground horse.

As the music starts to swirl, a smile spreads across
her face. She knows that she is back in charge of the
situation. Mirrored in her sunglasses are the figures

of the dark-haired boy and the Chinese girl hurrying through the crowds, clearly intent on something other than a fun day out.

Strike now? Or wait?

Wait a bit more. Somewhere quieter. Savor the control. Those two hired goons are nowhere to be seen, of course. Waste of space.

The carousel starts to spin. Her horse begins to rise and fall slowly. Her bag is heavier than normal, and she adjusts it on her shoulder. Better not to drop the thing! *I won't drop it. I'm in control—*

But then, as if from nowhere, a burst of that stupid laughter comes rising up out of her throat.

Why now? she thinks, fighting to regain her composure. *What would your old man say?* Everything's fine. You've got them where you want them, and it's just up to you when you plant the device. She breathes as deeply as she can, gripping the reins of her coal-black horse, knuckles whitening, and waits for the attack to pass.

22

WHY ROBOTS DO AS THEY'RE TOLD

Danny and Sing Sing jog through the fairground, past the Ferris wheel, past the carousel and the fast-food stalls. Ahead they can see the red airplane. Danny recognizes it from the photo, its red, chubby fuselage circling on a long boom arm, swinging out over the wooded hillside and then arcing back again to its take-off point. Happy faces of passengers are just visible in the portholes as it flies over their heads—presumably ignorant of the grisly discovery made here just a few days ago. One person who didn't enjoy their ride.

"Let's be quick," Danny says. "Before those hoodies make it up here."

"What are we looking for?" Sing Sing pants, struggling to keep up.

"We know he was either killed here or dumped here. Maybe we can spot a clue that the police missed."

Sing Sing glances over her shoulder. "You look for clues. I'll watch for lowlifes."

An elevated walkway juts over the hillside below. As they race out onto it, Danny's eyes are dragged to the view, the now distant Sagrada Familia. Beyond, the sea shines like beaten metal. Beautiful. Was this the last thing that the dead man saw? Does that make it better or worse, an image like that filling your eyes, but knowing that your end is about to come? His mind trips, and for a moment he's wondering what Mum and Dad thought, saw, felt as the fire engulfed them—

Leave it alone, he commands himself. *Nothing good comes of imagining that stuff. So drop it, numbskull.*

The plane thrums over their heads, its propeller whisking the blue sky. He looks up to follow its flight path, then back down to scan the ground under it. Below the walkway there's another level, with signs for a hall of mirrors and a robot museum.

"The police must have checked this level thoroughly," he says. "Let's try the one below. Something might have fallen down there. Or been chucked."

He drops down the stairwell two steps at a time. People are lining up for the hall of mirrors, its first concaved and fragmented panels stretching them or splitting them into pieces. Next to that, through the open door of the automaton museum, Danny can see small figures, jerkily animated, going through their paces as visitors feed coins into the antique slot machines. There's a hysterically laughing clown rocking in his glass case. Grotesque. And, next to that, a group of acrobats forming up into a pyramid. And next to that a model of the fairground itself, with tiny figures on the miniature rides. Everything running like clockwork. All strangely familiar—but disturbing too.

Between the two buildings there's a narrow gouge of a space. Danny glances up as the plane circles again, directly overhead.

It's worth a try. If something *was* dropped, it might've ended up down here. He shimmies into the gap as Sing Sing joins him.

"Keep watch," he says and squeezes into the gloomy passage.

"OK. But be quick!"

As soon as his eyes are accustomed to the dark, he's down on his hands and knees, ignoring the whiff of damp leaves and moldering food, crawling forward through the chucked Styrofoam cartons, windblown leaves and tissues.

Something bright ahead. He hurries forward to see what it is and finds an almost pristine cigarette packet, its cellophane wrapping crackling, reflecting the light. Only two cigarettes missing. Judging by its state, it can't have been down here long, and who throws away a nearly full packet of anything? Only if they're trying to quit—or are trying to hide some evidence. He turns it over excitedly in his hands. *This must be the pack the killer used to burn the marks into the man's back! Maybe there're prints on it . . . should have put some gloves on.*

And then he sees the matchbox just an arm's length away.

It burns in the gloom like a hot coal, a stylized tiger on the label, its rusty orange-and-black stripes burning fiercely. *I've seen it before*, he thinks, picking the box up with fingertips and holding it to the light. *But where?*

"What have you got?" Sing Sing calls impatiently, peering into the gloom.

Danny rolls the box over. Stamped on the back in bold black and orange type are the words: CLUB TIGRESSA, MONTJUÏC.

Of course! Javier's place! The same matchbox that I saw on Rosa's table . . .

The plane *thwumps* loudly overhead again, its shadow blocking the thin shaft of light, plunging Danny briefly into heavier shadow. "We're leaving!" he shouts down the alley.

"Back to the cathedral?"

"No, to Montjuïc. To ask Javier some questions." And, as he rejoins Sing Sing in the afternoon sunshine, he holds the box up triumphantly and rattles the matches inside.

The woman's ride on the black horse is coming to an end, the carousel slowing.

She stands on the stirrups, straining to see what's happened to the boy. And then she smiles.

There he is, emerging from the shadows between the hall of mirrors and the automaton museum. He's got something in his hand, showing it excitedly to the girl—and then the two of them go hurrying back toward the entrance. Must have found the cigarettes, the matchbox. Stupid police must have missed them! If that's the case, then they'll go looking for that deadbeat club owner now. Couldn't be better.

No trace of the nervous laughter now. *Because I'm in charge*, she thinks. *The boy thinks he's one step ahead, but it's time to strike.*

And I know just the place!

23

WHY YOU MIGHT SMEAR HONEY ON A MIRROR

The matchbox rattles in Danny's hand as they make their way out of the crowded fairground. It could be a coincidence, of course, but finding it and the discarded cigarette packet so close to where the body was dumped suggests that Javier may know far more than he's letting on. One thing's for sure. They need to confront him—and quickly.

Sing Sing takes out her wallet as they hurry across the Tibidabo parking lot. She peers into the billfold compartment, trying to look nonchalant, but it's clear from the twist of her mouth that funds are running low.

"We could walk it," Danny says, nodding at the wallet.

"Are you kidding? It would take us all afternoon. And there's plenty more where that came from—when business is settled back home."

"You should tell me about it, Sing Sing," Danny says. "I want to help."

"Appreciate it," Sing Sing says, her voice clipped. "Maybe later." The way she says it, though, sounds like "never."

She jumps into a waiting cab, tapping the driver on the shoulder. "Hey, you know a Club Tigressa? On Montjuïc?"

"Traffic very bad," the man says. "I drop you at cable car station. OK?"

Danny nods to the driver. "That's fine, thanks. Listen, Sing Sing, I could help if—"

She shakes her head. "No!" Her voice is like a pistol shot, but then she turns to him, smiling to soften the refusal. "Listen, we've got more immediate trouble, right? Javier. I mean, how well do you know him?"

"Not at all, really, but the Major thinks he's fine. More than fine. They seem like really old friends."

There are two versions of Javier playing in Danny's head now. On the one hand, the longtime friend of the company, a devoted family man, who tried to warn Zamora of the shifted cannon, who has seemed kind and supportive. On the other is a Javier who spent time in prison for killing another human being, who swam the murky waters of Barcelona, whose face has been fending off fear ever since Danny arrived.

Dad used to do that card trick with an outsized version of the king of clubs, changing its proud stare to a jolly smile and back again with a sweep of the hand. Two-faced king, he called it. But which is the real face? And now this evidence at the crime scene? Could Javier possibly have killed the young man— or burned the dots into his back? Maybe Javier's part of the Forty-Nine himself?

But surely Zamora couldn't be that wrong about someone, could he? Danny's thoughts turn to his old friend. He's always thought of the Major as being rock solid, dependable. But what with the secrecy over the reunion, the bad temper, a bad call or two in Hong Kong—well, in the end you have to admit that everyone is flawed, Zamora included. So maybe he could be wrong about Javier. Or holding something back again.

The car slams over a pothole, jarring Danny from the train of thought. Sing Sing's looking at him expectantly. "Let's look at your dad's flipping code on the way. What have we got?"

"You're right. Perhaps it'll give us a clue before we even get to Javier."

He pulls the paper from his pocket, spreading it out again, pen poised over the string of numbers. But then he hesitates. It's as if Dad's about to speak, after all—from beyond the grave, the first words he's spoken since the fire. And they'll be some of the last he will utter too.

Maybe it would be better to do this in private, Danny thinks. After all, the message could say anything. It could say something really silly and pointless, which would be embarrassing. Or it could be something that will change Danny's life once again. He looks at the handwriting—just that little bit more ragged than usual, and the heavy underlining is fierce. It has to mean something vital.

"Or do it on your own," Sing Sing says, as if guessing his reason for hesitating. Her eyes are almost devouring the paper and the half grid they already have.

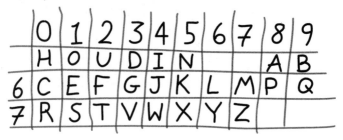

"OK, OK. Let's do it."

He looks again at what they have, checking that the letters are sitting in the right places, nothing duplicated. *Now we read. What do we have for the first word?*

7270271724563

"So anything starting with a seven or six is a double. You go to the row seven and read across to column two, which gives us T. Seventy gives R . . ."

He works quickly now, any need for privacy swept aside by the rush of excitement and anxiety as he starts to pick apart the letters. Sing Sing leans over, her hair falling across her face, masking the emotion there, but her body taut with anticipation. The world outside the taxi has fallen away—all of their focus now on this message from the past, from beyond the grave.

"T R U S T I N G—Here, you read me the numbers." He's working fast now, spelling out the message:

"Trusting E V E R Y T H I N G V I T A L T O M Y M E M O R Y P A L A C E. Then he's put that ampersand . . ."

"What's a memory palace?" Sing Sing cuts in.

"It's a way of remembering things quickly." Danny pauses, looking out at the city sweeping past. Again, he remembers Dad's voice, the spike of enthusiasm when he turned to his pet subjects, eager to explain, share—even if no one wanted to listen. Not always welcome, but now, how he misses it! "Dad used it all the time to store information, from card tricks to shopping lists. You think of a building—real or imaginary—and you have a number of rooms or things in it that you visit in order. And when you have to remember a pack of cards or a list of names, you quickly run around your memory palace in your head and put the objects in the rooms, making really strong mental pictures."

"I don't get it. Don't you end up with twice as much to remember?"

"You use the same memory palace for years, so you know it as well as your own home. Then, if your first place in the memory palace is a huge flight of steps—and the first thing you have to remember is *fish*, say—you quickly make a picture in your mind of fish flopping down the stairs. Or a fish bent like a flight of stairs. Then in the second place—it might be a mirror—you have to remember *honey*, so you imagine honey smeared all over the glass . . ."

"And what was *his* memory palace?"

"I don't know!" Danny says, exasperated. "But I know it had thirteen main places, with four sub-divisions in each. So that he could work card decks quickly."

The taxi is braking.

"*Montjuïc Teleferic,*" the driver says. "*Ocho euros.*"

They're on the flank of a low hill now—Montjuïc—the last fold of land before the sea. The taxi has pulled up at the bottom station of a cable car. Its pylons stalk the hillside, like a giant striding up and over public gardens, graveled paths, play areas, before making a sharp turn right and climbing to the castle at the top. A flow of bubble-like cabins loops down into the station, through the building, and then dances away again into the bright air.

This late in the season many of the cars are empty, and there's hardly any line at the ticket machine, just three teenagers feeding money into the barrier, and a solitary woman waiting immediately in front of them.

The woman's wearing a lime-green coat. She seems slightly out of breath and glances over her shoulder as Danny and Sing Sing approach from behind.

The teenagers climb noisily into an empty cabin as it shuffles around the platform, and the doors close automatically behind them.

"Let's make sure we get one to ourselves," Sing Sing whispers.

The woman in front turns around again, her heavy black shoulder bag banging against Danny.

"Oh, I'm sorry," she says. Her sunglasses are mirrored, reflecting the boy and girl in front of her. "You have the next one. It'll give me time to get my breath back," she adds with a smile.

"Thanks," Danny says. "We *are* in a hurry." Bit strange, though. The woman's obviously rushed to get there and then let them go in front.

"And I've got all the time in the world," the woman says.

The next car is turning through the station, and Danny and Sing Sing hop on board. The car sways as Danny throws himself on the seat and spreads out the code sheet again, eager now for the second part of Dad's message.

"*Adéu!*" The woman shouts a Catalan farewell as the doors clunk shut, and then she gives the cabin an encouraging whack.

"Phew," Sing Sing sighs, "glad she wasn't in our

cabin. Nice to have it to ourselves."

Danny nods, looking back—and is surprised to see that the woman has turned and is walking away from the terminus.

Something different about her as she goes?

"Must have changed her mind, I guess."

"Code, Danny," Sing Sing says, tapping the paper. The cable car rumbles on its guide rail and then is free, floating up in virtual silence, a bubble dragged on its thick high-tension wire, gaining height quickly as they head for a tall pylon marked *1*.

But Danny has no eyes for the view, his gaze trained on the next string of numbers. *Come on, Dad, say something useful,* he thinks. *Say something that's going to help me. Say something that's wise or helpful or makes me feel better—or tells me what on earth is going on! For all I know you've got three more sentences to make sense of my life again.*

"OK, let me have the next numbers."

Sing Sing calls out the digits, and Danny reads them off the rail fence grid. With an occasional stumble, he quickly adds letter to letter until the message is played out.

ASK Z ABOUT THE LAST PLACE CHECK IT FOR REAL.

"That's it?" Sing Sing asks, and this time there's no masking the disappointment in her voice.

"That's it for this one. Z must be Zamora, of course. And he must know something about Dad's memory palace."

"But how can you check a memory palace for real? If it's imaginary, I mean?"

"Because some people use real places as their models, right? Maybe Zamora knows where this place is . . ." But if Danny's honest, he too is disappointed. Not exactly a solid bit of evidence. No smoking gun. No greater understanding. *Typical Dad!* he thinks. *Nothing straightforward.*

Sing Sing's shoulders sag, her energy also draining. "What about the second code?"

"He hasn't broken that into words, so it's going to be a bit harder. And we need to crack the key first. *It's all around us. Always. Latin.*"

"Any ideas?"

"Not yet."

The cable car is already way above the hillside, shaking over pylons and then gliding the long intervals between. Below, just one or two people are making their way up the paths between the bushes and trees, but otherwise, the place is almost deserted.

A slight sea breeze comes whispering through the little window high up in their cabin. They're all alone.

"What's always around us? Air?" Sing Sing wonders. "Trouble?" she adds gloomily. "What's the Latin for air?"

"Don't know. We were about to start Latin next term at school."

They're approaching the halfway station now. A set of giant yellow wheels grabs each car in turn, shifting it through a right angle and then launching it once again toward the summit of Montjuïc. The car with the teenagers makes its turn, and then Danny and Sing Sing go rattling through the mechanism, spat out of the winding gear and lifted quickly up again to more than a hundred feet above the ground, floating in the sunshine. The shadow of their car looks very small as it slips across the graveled play area below.

"It'll come to me," Danny says. "It'll come. Just got to think like Dad . . ."

But again, he's wondering just how easy that is. Dad—the mystery-monger, as Darko used to call him—seems more and more like a stranger now. If Dad has a Hu, or whatever Sing Sing called it, it's certainly a difficult one to get to know.

A piercing screech fills the cabin, making Danny jump. The cable car judders to a halt, sending them both sliding from the seat.

"What now?" Sing Sing wails.

On the wall above, a Spanish voice is delivering its automated alarm message from the speaker.

For a moment the car swings on its hook, the rocking motion giving way to an uneasy stillness, as they hang, marooned exactly halfway between the pylons, maybe a hundred feet or more from each. Below, a handful of children are standing in the play area, pointing up at the motionless cars above, their voices and laughter floating on the breeze.

Danny gets up and jabs the red alarm call button.

"Hello? *Hola*?! We're stuck. *Hola*?"

And then another sound fills the cabin. A familiar ringtone: so familiar but so unexpected that it takes him a full ten seconds to realize what he's hearing. It's the opening bars of Billy's version of "Expressway to Your Skull"—the one Danny recorded on that last tour and set as a ringtone on his phone.

But it can't be! he thinks. *I lost it, didn't I?*

Sing Sing's looking at her coat pocket, confused. Because that's where the ringtone is coming from.

She reaches in and pulls out a cell phone, holding it out and looking bewildered.

"I don't have a phone with me," she says. "Is it yours?"

"Can't be! I lost mine."

But it certainly looks like his.

24

WHY SAFETY CAN'T ALWAYS COME FIRST

Danny takes the phone gingerly, as if it might bite, the chiming guitar refrain still ringing.

"I lost it," he says, "so how did it end up in your pocket?"

"No flipping idea. Answer it, dummy!"

He slides the lock and taps the Answer icon. "Hello?"

"*Hola*, Danny," a woman's voice says. It sounds strangely familiar, a voice he's heard recently, but he can't place it at once. "Are you having a nice ride with your friend?"

"Who is this?"

"I'm just calling with a message," the voice goes on. The tone is flat, even, as if the speaker wants to take all emotion from her voice.

"What message? Who are you?" He holds the phone away from his ear, punching the Speaker icon to let Sing Sing hear.

"Do you know what a nemesis is, Danny? It's the person who deals you your fate. I am your nemesis, the person who kills you. I am the person who has clamped a bomb to the side of your cable car. A little bit of Semtex makes a very big bang indeed."

He sees it all now, in a moment.

The woman at the bottom station, the one with the green coat. The same green he saw in the cathedral last night! She bumped into them—must have dropped the phone into Sing Sing's coat pocket then—and that thwacking sound when she hit the car was her planting the device. He scrunches his eyes shut, struggling to recall what had caught his attention as she walked away. That's it—when she turned she had no bag on her shoulder.

"You're just trying to scare us," Sing Sing shouts back.

"Clock's ticking," the flat voice says, her tone sharpening. "Just thought you should have a minute or two. Say your good-byes! Then it's mutilation time."

Silence in the cabin now.

"Hello? Are you still there?" Danny shouts.

"I have to go," the woman says. "But I hope you notice I stopped you between pillar twelve and thirteen. The highest drop on the route. *Adéu.*"

The line goes dead.

"It's gotta be a joke, right?" Sing Sing says.

Danny looks at the phone in his hands. He fumbles for the call records. One incoming call is listed as NUMBER WITHHELD. The address book is blank. The phone's memory seems to have been wiped. What now? He can't remember Zamora's number. And no point calling emergency services— not enough time.

He's in no doubt that what the woman says is true, but he feels curiously calm all of a sudden. *If this is the end, then fair enough, they got me. But I'm not going down without a fight. And I'm not letting Sing Sing die here in this stupid tin can.* He looks up at the roof of their cabin, the gap to the next pylon, grappling for solutions.

"It's no joke," Danny says. "We're getting out of here."

In the movies there's always a hatch in the roof, but this one's solid. He clambers up onto the seat, setting their bubble rocking again, struggling to open the air vent at the top of the window.

"Reckon we could get through this," he says through gritted teeth, "if I can get it open." Sing Sing hops up beside him. She takes two breaths right down inside her, another one deeper still, her shoulder loosening, knuckles contracting, and then, with a hiss of air between her teeth, strikes with her right hand, unleashing a blow that pops the vent from its hinges and sends it cartwheeling to the ground below.

"I've got an idea," she says, turning her oval face to the uphill wire, gazing at the incline as if mesmerized by it.

But Danny isn't listening. *So do I*, he thinks, pulling the carabiner from his jeans pocket and looking at it carefully, unscrewing the gate, checking it for cracks. After all, it had a hefty blow when it hit the stone floor of the Sagrada, and Frankie had tossed it for good reason. "Safety foist and second and thoid and last," he would drawl in an exaggeration of his Brooklyn accent. But what about when you have no choice?

"If we can get on the roof, we can put this on the wire," he says hurriedly. "Then run my belt through, make a loop, and hang from it. Go down like a zipwire. I saw Archaos do an act like that at a festival . . . kind of . . ." His voice trails off, still trying to convince himself of the plan. "Then we can climb down the ladder."

"I don't know that it would hold us both," Sing Sing says, working her way up into the space where the vent was. "I think it's time for my audition."

Her eyes are on the cable, a focus that is even more intense than he's seen in her before.

"What?"

"Ever heard of the *oribat*? The *neurobat*? The *funambule*?"

"They're all words for wire walkers."

"That's my act, Danny. Well, kinda. That's my trick. My surprise."

"You're a wire walker?"

"Slack-wire acrobat. But I can do this. I think." With a quick pull of her arms, she's half out of the narrow opening, then twisting, feet scrabbling for purchase. Danny grabs hold of one of her flailing feet and anchors it for her—and she's gone.

Danny's stomach is turning, but once again, he can feel his system tingling with that good feeling: the return of that adrenaline, the knowledge that you're about to do something that might be better not done, the realization that there's no going back.

But how long have we got? he thinks.

Sing Sing extends an arm from her precarious perch on the roof. "Get a flipping move on!"

It's Danny's turn to wriggle, twist, pivot his way out of the cabin. His right hand grabs the cabin roof, his left a firm circus grip with Sing Sing, and he pulls as she pulls, his feet treading empty air, then the soles of his shoes gripping a window ledge—and he's up, panting with the effort.

Their world is now a small metal roof, sun-splashed, surrounded by that peculiar emptiness of a vertigo-inducing drop. A stubby hook rises from the center of the cable car, about the height of his head, and from that the wire runs away steeply in both directions, downhill to pylon 12, up to number 13.

"Let's use the carabiner," he says, trying to nail the right tone, to persuade Sing Sing to go with his plan. "You can't walk that! You'd need a decent balance pole, wouldn't you? And that angle!"

"I can do it," Sing Sing says quietly. "It's just a death walk. And you don't know if that ring will hold. Or your belt. Especially with two of us on it.

Now get a flipping move on and leave me to do my own thing!"

He goes to argue, then sees it's useless. She's as gripped by her own idea as he is by his.

"Good luck, then." He pats her awkwardly on the shoulder, and she flashes him a smile.

"Get going, dummy."

Sing Sing pulls herself up onto the hook mechanism, kicking off her shoes, throwing them to the ground below. She looks very much like she knows what she's doing—or is making her best effort to convince both Danny and herself that she won't simply take one step and fall.

The children below—and their parents—are watching now with rapt attention, aware that something very odd is happening. Faces trained their way, eyes shielded from the sun.

Danny works fast now. He rips the belt from his jeans and reaches up to the thick wire on the downhill side of the hook. With some difficulty, he forces it through the carabiner's open jaw. Just a fraction to spare—thank the stars. And then he's tightening the screw lock with quick fingers. Behind him, he's aware Sing Sing is already standing on top of the hook, her arms out, stilling her body, finding the one point where her center of gravity, the weight of the earth, the tight wire, all line up in a perfect balance. He can't help but watch, her actions snaring his attention despite their race against the clock.

"I'm going," she says quietly, and then—it's breathtaking, terrifying, beautiful as she commits herself to the wire. She lifts her foot, points her toes, brings it down on the cable in front of her, slides it forward, then quickly lifts the other foot from its place of safety, points, places, slides, edging out across the empty space below her.

He watches her for five full precious seconds, his heart firing with elation and dread. He knows that without a pole it will be so much harder for her to keep her center of gravity inside the "magic box" over the wire. Once she loses that—it doesn't bear thinking about. *And this cable will be greased too*, he thinks. *Mum always cleaned the oil off a new wire. It must be incredibly slippery.*

But still she goes, her arms making quick precise adjustments, like someone sending signals. And then her voice comes dancing back along the wire. "Get moving, you idiot!"

Danny snaps back to his own plight, threading

the belt through the metal ring, looping it, wrapping his wrists through that, and binding himself tightly to the wire. *Got to trust that carabiner,* he thinks, *got to hope it's not about to snap.*

He lets his knees sag, allowing his weight to come onto the makeshift zipwire mechanism, testing it. *Seems OK. So let's go.*

His feet take a bit of weight back, as he shuffles to the edge of the cabin roof, ready for launch. One last look behind him. Sing Sing's about halfway across the gap, moving more quickly, her eyes still fixed on the top of the next pylon, climbing above and away from him.

Then he pushes off. Immediately gravity has hold of him, full force. There's hardly any resistance, and the carabiner goes screaming down the wire, accelerating so fast that it takes him by surprise, sending him twisting, the leather of his belt digging deep into his hands and wrists, his arms tugging in their sockets. *Got to get it back under control.* With all his strength he steadies the spin, his body turning again toward the lower pylon.

It's only now that he realizes the problem. In a second or two he will be smashed against it at full speed.

He twists hard, jamming the carabiner sideways against the wire, setting off a shower of sparks, a squeal of metal on metal.

Still too fast.

Pulling with his arms, hitch-kicking from the waist as if turning on a trapeze, he brings his feet up, jamming the soles of his shoes against the wire, pushing with the last of his energy, feeling the lactic acid build and burn his muscles.

Too late?

No. His efforts are just enough. There's a stench of hot rubber from the bottom of his shoes and then, with a thump that jars the air out of him, he slams into the pillar and hangs there for a moment, his feet scrabbling for the security of the rungs set into the side of the pylon.

Got them. Now what? And how's Sing Sing?

Behind him the cable car still dangles serenely from the stilled wire. Maybe it was a hoax after all. Maybe the woman was just trying to scare them. *At least that's the Hanged Man business over and done with,* he thinks, remembering the tarot cards and seeing again that calm smile on the inverted man's face.

Beyond the cable car he can see his friend, just a few more paces from safety. He watches her, willing her to keep centered, to keep moving. When—if!—this bomb goes off, it will shake her to the ground for sure. He remembers that footage of Karl Wallenda, the high-wire king, plummeting to his death, the grainy images depicting the last moments before his fall, the tumble into space, into nothingness.

Sing Sing wobbles.

A massive lurch of her body. Her right leg shoots out to counterbalance, her fingers splaying like birds of prey.

No! Stay on the wire.

Danny wants to look away—but can't. Just like he couldn't stop himself from rewatching the YouTube video of Wallenda's death.

He feels sick to his stomach as he unknots his hands and grips the metal rungs of the ladder that's clamped to the side of the pylon. He looks down briefly, checking his foothold—and then it happens.

A simultaneous blast of heat, light, and sound as the mechanism detonates. The explosion pushes him flat against the ladder, so hot he wonders if his hair will catch fire, little pieces of safety glass striking his body, pinging off the metal pylon. The bang so loud it sets his ears pulsing.

He looks back.

A fireball rolls up and around the stricken cabin, turning in on itself, the flame engulfing the hook and the wire—blocking the view of Sing Sing beyond. There are screams from the children and parents below as they scurry away from under the blast.

Black smoke replaces the flame now, coughing up from the wreck of the car. Miraculously it's still clinging to the wire. The sides have been peeled away by the blast, twisted metal curled back, and the whole thing is hanging at an angle. Unearthly noises come singing down the high tension wire to Danny, amplifying through the pylon, like distressed whale calls from out of the depths.

Where's Sing Sing? Not a sign of her. His eyes race along the empty wire, down pylon 13, across the ground, scanning for her stricken body, broken on the hard earth.

Is that her? No, it's a man, crouched down, covering his head to protect himself from falling debris.

The cable car twitches on the wire. He can feel its terminal shake reach down to his pylon, setting it vibrating.

And then, with a ripping of metal, the cabin separates from the hook and falls, trailing flame and smoke, turning a slow half somersault in the air before slamming into the ground roof first, flattening on impact.

She can't have made it to the pylon in time. She must have fallen, he thinks desperately.

And he has never felt so alone.

25

WHY YOU SHOULD ALWAYS LOOK TWICE

For a moment Danny can't move. His feet are rooted to the steps of the ladder, hands locked solid, oblivious now to the drop below. He swallows hard, biting back grief. She must have fallen into those trees, but surely it's too much to hope she can have survived that.

If that's the case—if Sing Sing *has* fallen—then how on earth will he have the strength to go on? It's hard to put into words, but somehow, life's made a bit more sense since he met her. As if a void has been filled . . .

Smoke from the broken cable car wafts over him, stinging his eyes. He closes them, blinking rapidly, seeing nothing for a moment, just hearing the sound of children crying in the park below and, beyond that, sirens already curdling the air at the foot of Montjuïc. She can't be taken from him now . . .

. . . and then he hears her voice.

"I flipping did it, Danny! I DID IT!"

There she is, clinging to the outside of the doors of the teenagers' undamaged cable car, then working her way toward the pylon, onto the ladder, and down.

The relief is immediate, jolting energy back into his tired arms and legs, setting a crazy grin on his face. He loosens his grip on the rungs and then starts to tap his way down, feet ringing on each step, gravity and his own body strength propelling him to the bottom as quickly as possible. *She's OK, she's OK*, he repeats to himself as he goes. *She's flipping well OK!*

The bottom fifteen rungs are shielded by an anti-climb panel, but he simply jumps it. He lands hard, stumbling, losing his balance and rolling twice on the ground. To his amazement Sing Sing is already at the bottom of his pylon and looking down at him. A grin on her face too.

"How'd you get down so fast?"

"Mine was a lot shorter."

"I thought you'd run out of time!"

"Worst one I've ever done," she says, shaking

her head, the grin disappearing—and he suddenly sees she is shaking all over. "I ran the last few steps. Horrible!"

"We did it."

"Yep. We did." Her fists are clenching and unclenching, the thrill and fear still alive in her body.

"Let's get away from here. In case that woman's still around. And I don't want to talk to the police."

"Who was she?" Sing Sing shouts as they run up through the bushes toward the road to the castle.

"She must be with the Forty-Nine. I'm sure she was the woman in the cathedral tower yesterday."

"Where are we going?"

"We'll get across this road, then hide in the park on the other side," Danny says, shoes clawing the ground, eager to be away from the site of the explosion, to buy them some time.

He's reached the empty service road and excitedly glances over his shoulder, back at Sing Sing, willing her to hurry.

"Maybe she's even the boss of the Forty-Nine—the Center. We kept thinking it was a man . . ." he continues, and fails to see the little red sports car cornering hard, powering its way down the hill toward the city, its engine snarling.

"DANNY!"

Sing Sing's anguished shout snaps him back to the moment, but he knows his movements are way too slow. He sees the sports car so late that, unable to decide whether to go forward or back, he simply stays fixed to the spot, watching the car skid toward him, its wheels locking, the driver's hands visible now, working hard to control the spin, the sound of the tires black-striping the tarmac. The car's tail drifts slowly out, a red wall coming at him sideways—and he braces for impact, cursing himself for being so stupid.

But the vehicle continues its spin and blows past, missing him by next to nothing, the backdraft tugging at his clothes, before completing one full revolution. The driver pumps the brakes and straightens it up, before thumping into the curb and coming to a jarring halt.

"Maniac!" Sing Sing screams and stomps down the road ready to confront the driver. "What the—!"

Her voice cuts short as the car door opens and Javier's heavy figure squeezes from the Alfa Romeo. "Danny! Are you OK?"

"You nearly killed him!" Sing Sing shrieks, taking a step toward the Catalan. For a moment Danny is pretty sure she's going to kick him, and he hurries to her side, holding her back.

"Sing Sing, it was my fault!"

"What are you doing up here?" Javier says, quickly surveying the street, the parks to either side. "What was that explosion?"

"Someone tried to kill us," Danny says, feeling surprisingly calm as he gazes into Javier's eyes. *Perhaps the surprise will give me an advantage*, he thinks. If Javier really is involved with this whole business, maybe he'll give himself away or can be persuaded. Try another hypnotic snap induction like the one on Tony in Hong Kong.

But Javier can't return the stare. He looks away, screwing his eyes up tight.

The sirens are gathering at the bottom of the hill, and there's the steady rhythmic pulse of a helicopter buffeting the air, presumably on the way to investigate the cable car explosion.

"We have to get out of here," Javier says quietly. "We have to get out of here, right now. Get in my car. Quickly."

"Not until you answer me one question."

"We've *got* to go, Danny!"

"Who is the woman in the green coat?"

Javier looks around again helplessly, then turns back to Danny. "Get in the car and I'll tell you everything I know."

"Don't trust him, Danny," Sing Sing barks.

"I promise you I'll take you straight back to the Mysterium," Javier says, already moving toward the Alpha Romeo. "I promise on my kids' lives."

"Let's go then," Danny says and runs for the car.

Javier backs the car up, his hand on the gear stick shaken by more than the engine's growl. He points the Alfa downhill once again and accelerates hard, wheels biting for tarmac.

"Are we running from the police? Or the Forty-Nine?" Danny asks as they fly around a curve and then go bumping across a junction, cutting down a steep backstreet toward Paral·lel Avenue and El Raval.

"Both."

Ahead there's standing traffic lining the side street, waiting to try and get out into the jam on the main road beyond. Javier brings the Alfa back down the gears, glancing in the rearview mirror, his body relaxing just a little bit.

"I found a matchbox for the Tigressa," Danny says. "It was up at Tibidabo. Under the airplane ride. There were cigarettes too—I think they were used to burn the dots into that man's back."

"A lot of people use my club—" Javier starts to say and then clams up tight.

"But there's something you're feeling really bad about," Danny says, tapping the steering wheel with his hand to get Javier's attention. "I know it. You're desperate to tell me something, but you can't bring yourself to do it. Why?"

Javier sighs and then brings the car to a halt, bumping it up onto the curb just short of the stalled traffic ahead. He puts the car into neutral and yanks on the hand brake.

He shuts his eyes again, very tightly. That's the clincher, Danny knows, that's guilt for sure. He can't look at what he's done, not even inwardly. He's trying to avoid it—but it's eating away at him.

"What is it?" Danny asks softly.

"It was my fault. Zamora's accident. My fault," Javier groans.

"Why?" Sing Sing snaps from the backseat.

"Because—because *I* moved the marks on the floor. After Zamora and Frankie had measured it all."

Danny nods. "And at the last minute you tried to warn him?"

Javier groans. "*Si. Si.* At least he's going to be OK, but he could have been killed—"

"But why, Javier?" Danny searches out the man's face. "Why hurt Zamora?"

Javier opens his eyes, and when he does, they are filled with such sorrow, such remorse, that the pain is almost too much to witness. "Because they're threatening my family. My kids. Lope. The Forty-Nine have me like that." He clenches his fist up tight.

"And who is the woman in the green coat? With that weird laughter?"

"That woman?" He shakes his head. "That, Danny—that is La Loca."

"Loca?"

"The Madwoman. She's a hired killer. Professional. One of the most feared assassins all around this end of the Mediterranean. And you're her current target. And it's partly my fault, may heaven forgive me."

A police car frees itself from the traffic ahead and comes thumping up the side street, siren howling, closely followed by another.

"Maybe the police will get her," Danny says hopefully, but he knows as he says it that he's clutching at straws.

Javier shakes his head. "She comes from a long line of contract killers. She's never been caught. Never failed. But they say that once or twice—when people nearly got away—she just loses control, and all the emotion and rage come out of her in that horrible laugh . . . It's the last thing you hear."

Danny swallows hard. He's heard that laughter, and the memory of it puts a chill through him.

"What happened on the cable car?" Javier asks, his voice so quiet you can hardly hear it.

"Doesn't matter. It's not important now. I need to know everything you can tell me about the Forty-Nine, Javier. Anything at all."

"I don't know where to start."

"Try."

Javier sighs. "Remember my photo of us all, back in the old days, the Velázquez painting?"

Danny nods, holding his impatience back.

"Picasso did forty or more versions of it. He was obsessed with it too. Some are almost abstract, some leave out figures or change the way they stood but all recognizably the same picture—"

"Answer his question, dummy. We don't want a flipping lecture!" Sing Sing says, banging the seat.

But Javier ignores her. "One of them, my favorite, is black and white. That dark figure in the lit doorway just . . . takes your breath away." He opens his eyes wide. "So powerful. So mysterious. It's just like the situation we've got. A mysterious figure, no?"

Danny can hear his own heartbeat now in the silence of the car. "And?"

"Each major country or region has its local representative—the sector chief of the Forty-Nine. Those people are referred to by a number and a ringed dot on the diagram. The closer that dot is to the center—to *the* Center—the higher the number. The sector head here is numbered 38."

"And that person's in the Mysterium?"

"No. But someone associated with the Mysterium is heavily involved with the Forty-Nine."

"Who? WHO?!"

Javier's about to speak but hesitates, his eyes caught by something down the street, his mouth frozen, a syllable perched on his lips. Not a vowel, Danny thinks, definitely a consonant, lips pushed slightly forward and open. Something like a *J* or *D* or *T*.

"Who is it, Javier?"

But Javier's gaze suddenly recoils, as if he's been smacked in the face. Something in what he sees puts fear into the car, a palpable dread—and Danny turns to see what has caused it.

Moving through the packed crowds on Paral·lel is a bright flash of green, a swing of short, bleached hair. Then she's gone.

Without any consideration of the danger, Danny is out of the passenger door and tearing off down the side street.

"Danny? Come back!" Javier shouts.

But Danny's in no mood for listening. *I'm going to take the fight to them*, he thinks, running hard down the street. *I'm going to go on the attack.*

"Wait for me! Danny!" He can hear Sing Sing scrambling from the car and rushing to follow.

"Stay there," he shouts back. "Stay with Javier!"

He sprints down the street, out of the shadows, onto the chaos of Paral·lel, where the traffic is still snarled in a chorus of car horns. This side of the city seems to have ground to a halt.

Danny jumps up on top of a garbage can, scanning ahead like a lookout on a ship's mast.

"Wait!"

Sing Sing comes weaving through the crowd to join him.

"I said stay with Javier!"

"What are you doing?"

"I saw La Loca."

His eyes are roving the packed pavement, the crowds around the subway entrance up ahead.

Is that her? Just going down the steps under the big red *M* of the metro. Danny jumps from the garbage can, weaving, brushing shoulders with pedestrians, hurdling trailed suitcases, with Sing Sing close behind.

He plants a hand on the rail and leaps over the low wall, dropping the first flight of steps, eyes already scouring the tunnel ahead. Not a sign of that green coat . . .

"Lost her," he says as Sing Sing catches him.

"Let's try the platforms, then."

But there's no sign. They spend ten fruitless minutes combing the warren of Paral.lel station and then make their way quickly back up to the surface. The traffic's moving again, and the horns have subsided as they cover the ground back to Javier.

Turning up the darkened side street, though, there is still one horn blaring. A long, unbroken wail of a horn—and it's coming from Javier's Alfa.

"He's trying to warn us," Sing Sing shouts.

"I don't think so. You'd pump it fast. To make it sound urgent—"

Danny sprints up the street, running as fast as he can back toward the little red car and the small knot of people already clustering around it. Some are banging on the window, some looking more worried. One woman reels away holding her hand to her mouth, her eyes wide in shock.

In his gut, Danny already knows what he will find when he opens the door.

And so he's not taken completely off guard when he wrenches it open and sees Javier slumped forward, his big head heavy on the center of the steering wheel, his body motionless.

It does, though, take a moment to notice the long knife, buried almost up to its hilt in Javier's back— and the blood that's running thickly, darkly down the leather jacket. Whatever was on the tip of Javier's tongue will never be spoken now. Not by him.

The Alfa's horn blares on into the fading light.

ACT THREE

IN SPAIN THE DEAD ARE MORE ALIVE
THAN IN ANY OTHER COUNTRY IN
THE WORLD.

—*Frederico García Lorca*

26

WHY GOOD PEOPLE
DO BAD THINGS

Danny slumps on the backseat of the taxi, his mind numb.

It's like the worst bizarro day ever, he thinks. Once in every Mysterium tour there would be a date so disastrous, so cockeyed, that you simply had to forget it, chalk it up to experience and wait for the next day to dawn. A wind might spring up so fiercely that the big top couldn't be pitched. (Frankie: "Remember when Archaos got blown down in Dublin? That was the end for 'em.") Or a bad fall would send someone off to the emergency room. Or the show would play to a half-empty house. And Dad would bang into the trailer later that night; slump on the bench seat; and then pull his big hand across his face, as if trying to wipe the words and emotions away. He would sigh, and then the hand would drop to reveal a smile of sorts—a bit like the king of clubs trick—and he'd announce: "Well, that's that. That's bizarro day out of the way for this tour."

But now it feels like every single day is bizarro day. Far worse. Danny can't get the image of Javier's lifeless body from his head.

Still clutched tightly in Danny's hand is the piece of paper he pulled from Javier's jacket. It took a huge effort of will to unzip the dead man's pocket—and then palm the note in case anyone was looking. But he had to know what Lope's message said, what had made Javier flinch, no matter how wrong it felt to do it. He had taken a last look at the poor man slumped on his wheel, and then they had hurried from the scene.

Now Danny unfolds the note again and hands it to Sing Sing. The shock has taken the wind out of even her. And maybe she's still coming down from that high-wire buzz.

"*Zamora. 38*," she reads aloud, and raises her eyebrows. "What does it mean? You don't think the Major's . . . ?"

"No!" Danny says quickly, as if he doesn't even want the thought to be voiced. "No. I'm sure it was an order for Javier to act against Zamora. That's why he looked so awful when he read it." He leans back and closes his eyes. Groans. "I'm going to have to tell Zamora everything," he says.

"I reckon we should tell *everyone* everything."

"Just the Major for now. Remember Javier told us that a member of the company is involved—"

"Someone *around* the company," Sing Sing corrects. "I'm still thinking about this Jimmy T guy. Could he really be behind all this? Sounds like a flipping loser. I wish Javier had coughed up a bit more before he went and died on us."

Her voice is harder again. *A bit like that first day we met in the Golden Bat,* Danny thinks. *She's armoring herself again, so it's best if I keep as open as possible, make her feel we can trust each other—that we're stronger together than when we're each clamming up tight in our own defensive shells.*

"Javier was about to say a name, but he stopped when he saw that woman. He was making the shape of the first sound. It was a pushed consonant—I think it was probably a *J*, but I couldn't be sure."

"Joey?" Sing Sing prompts. "Or could it have been Jimmy?"

I don't know, he thinks. *I could be wrong.* But then a lot of other people are also getting things wrong. He thinks again of Javier, of his wife and children waiting for him to come home. *They're even younger than I was,* he thinks.

By the time they return to the Sagrada the light is fading over the city—a few bruised clouds against the pale sky and the cathedral's exterior spotlights already coming on, lighting the towers, the scaffolding, the cranes.

Zamora is waiting in the shadows on the steps to the main entrance. Tied to the railings to his right, a Mysterium banner shifts in the gathering breeze.

The Major leaps to his feet as soon as he sees them, his right arm strapped to his chest, hurrying toward them as best he can with a pronounced limp, his mouth already open, eager to get the first word.

"Mister Danny. Sing Sing. AT LAST! You've got to stay put and stop chasing around on your own. I waited for Javier, but he didn't come. Thought I'd better come and check that you were OK—"

"Major. I've got bad news," Danny says. He puts

his hand on Zamora's shoulder.

"Oh?" Zamora says, stopping short. The look on Danny's face tells him at once how serious it is. "I'm afraid that makes two of us."

———————————

Thirty minutes later, Zamora is sitting at a café table, staring vacantly into the thickening darkness outside. Danny follows his gaze, eyes drawn by the cathedral's spotlit towers, a single word glowing high up on one of them: *HOSANNA!*

He's wondering if he's broken the news in the best way. If he should have been less direct, softened the blow somehow. But there's no time to tiptoe around, is there? And the Major's got one or two things wrong himself!

Zamora's digesting the shocking news, absentmindedly stroking his plaster cast. A tear slides slowly, quietly from his left eye. He looks like he's aged ten years in a day, older and more distant suddenly. *As if he's retreating from me,* Danny thinks, *like there's a gap between us. I wonder how much I really do know him—even after all these years. Not quite the rock I always thought he was . . . ?*

"Poor Javier," the Major says quietly. "Poor Javier. I'm so sorry."

"But didn't you hear what Danny said?" Sing Sing says, reaching across the table and tugging at Zamora's good arm. "Javier tried to kill you! *He* moved the flipping cannon! He was in with the Forty-Nine!"

Stung by the words, the Major looks up fiercely, the tear a point of light on his cheek. "I heard that, Sing Sing. I heard it, OK? But what could he bleeding well do?"

"Warn you!"

"A parent would do anything to safeguard his children—"

Sing Sing shakes her head and looks away, rolling Cantonese under her breath.

"Javier did try to warn him," Danny says.

"That's right!" Zamora says, as much to himself as his companions. "And Javier and I were like *that* once." He twists his index and middle fingers tightly together, his hand shaking as he does so. "He saved my life in a fight in Barceloneta."

He wipes the tear away, putting strength back into his shoulders, squaring them. He glances up in the direction of Javier's apartment. "I'll have to go and tell Lope. Oh God . . ."

Danny reaches out across the table. "I'll come with you, if you like."

"No. Leave that to me."

"What about *your* bad news?" Danny says, steeling himself.

"*Carajo*! I forgot." Zamora swigs the last of his beer in one long pull. "You remember Laura was talking about some trouble?"

"Something to do with an old case?"

"*Sí.*" Zamora puffs out his cheeks. "Well, it's reached up and bitten her. She's been detained on a European arrest warrant. She's wanted in Italy for questioning about an unsolved murder."

Danny groans. "But she can't be involved in something like that!"

"Of course not. But it doesn't matter. Her lawyer told me these European warrants are carried out very quickly. She's in some police station in London, but she could be in Rome in days. Hours."

"I need to talk to her," Danny says, urgently. "The Forty-Nine must be involved. They must have links to the mafia, right? They're trying to get Laura out of the way."

"Doubt we can reach her, Danny. So I'm taking

charge. Acting guardian," Zamora says, getting awkwardly to his feet. "You two go and sit tight in the cathedral until I've seen Lope."

"I'm not sure we can trust anyone in there," Danny says firmly.

"Oh, come on now," Zamora grunts. "Rosa? Darko? Maria? Beatrice? Frankie?"

"Frankie let that light drop that nearly hit me," Danny says, counting off suspects, finger by finger. "Rosa was hiding something the night of the fire, Joey and Aki may have been involved in the water tank, and Jimmy T's name keeps coming up." He holds his hand up, all five fingers splayed for good effect.

"Danny, I would stake my life on the decency of the Mysterium's company. Your dad said as much—and he was an excellent judge, as I'm always saying. Rosa may have spiky corners, but she was there from the start—or shortly afterward—and Harry trusted her. That's good enough for me. Frankie just messed up with that light. We know who moved the cannon marks after all. And you've seen this assassin yourself. Maybe no one in the company—"

"Javier said someone in or around the company was involved," Danny repeats, tapping the table.

"And what should we do about this Loca woman?" Sing Sing says.

"Keep with everyone in the cathedral, Danny, and you should be safe enough for the next hour. Even if there *is* a rotten egg, they can't act in front of the others, can they? And then we'll get out of town. I know someone in Sitges who'll put us up—"

"But tomorrow's opening night!"

"Blast that!" Zamora snaps. "You're more important." He throws down some money for the drinks and limps for the door.

"Wait, Major!" Danny jumps up, pushing back his chair. "Do you know anything about Dad's memory palace?"

"Don't think we've got time to mess around—"

"I cracked Dad's first code. It mentions the memory palace. And you!"

Zamora stops in the doorway and scratches his head. "No idea what that's about—"

"But *where* was Dad's? What was his palace?"

"Stone's throw from here, as a matter of fact. Park Güell. The place that the great architect Gaudi designed, same time as he was drawing up that monster." Zamora points at the Sagrada. "There's a giant

263

lizard spouting water at the main gate, and you used to like sitting on it . . ."

"And do you know what the last memory point was in the park?" Danny presses, buoyed by the news that the memory palace is so close to hand.

"*Si, si.* We used to walk the same route every time, back when we were planning the Mysterium. We always ended up there. It's a spiral mound on a hill, with an amazing view from it. Why?"

"Doesn't matter," Danny says hurriedly, tugging Sing Sing by the arm. "We'll be in the Sagrada waiting for you."

As they hurry back across the road, Sing Sing turns impatiently to Danny. "But what about this Park Güell? The memory palace? We've got to see what's there!" Her eyes are bright with determination, her hands gesticulating, windmilling. "Don't give up now!"

"I'm not. We're going to get a flashlight from the prop store and get going. We can be back before the Major knows."

"Now you're talking!" Sing Sing beams and hurtles up the steps into the cathedral, renewed energy in her legs, leaving Danny a few paces behind. Something else is driving her determination, he thinks. She's taking it all very personally—of course someone has tried to kill her too—but it's taken some powerful force to pull her halfway around the world, something more than the promise of an audition.

He hurries after her into the hushed and darkened cathedral.

27

WHY MOSQUITOES CAN'T HELP BEING MOSQUITOES

The company members are taking a break at the far end of the nave, sitting around in ones and twos under the great vaulted roof, voices echoing in the near deserted building.

Izzy is balancing, star position, inside a Cyr wheel and spinning it slowly across the floor, the polished steel ring reflecting bright points of light. Danny follows them, glancing at the stairways twisting up into the darkness of the towers above—and feels the height, the weight, the chaos of the building towering over him. Whereas it felt uplifting on day one, now it simply feels overwhelming.

"We need to tell Rosa about Javier," Sing Sing says.

Danny shakes his head. "No. It would take too much time, and she'll find out anyway. And she might stop us from leaving. Let's just get going to the Güell."

And if I'm honest, he thinks, *I'm fed up with the lot of them anyway. No one's being straightforward.* His mounting anger is cutting against the fear now, the vulnerability.

Sing Sing is at his shoulder, watching his face. "You OK?"

"Still think you want to join this company?" he says.

"It does seem like a bit of a flipping nuthouse," she says, "but—"

"Nuthouse?!" a voice says from out of the gloom. It's Darko, sitting on a walking globe just outside the makeshift arena. Behind him in the shadows is the target for his Wheel of Life stunt, its concentric red and white circles notched by countless hits from the throwing knives. Darko's case lies open by his boots—all ten knives snug in their red-velvet-lined grooves.

Darko shakes his head. "My old dad always said the circus is an island of sanity in a sea of madness!"

Danny nods, impatient to get on to the Güell,

but the knife thrower reaches out and touches him lightly on the arm. "You've been through a lot, Danny. But don't give up."

"I'm not. I just need people to start telling me the truth!" The frustration fires the words out harder than Danny intends.

"We never know what's lurking in the shadows, do we?" Darko says, his eyes seeking out Danny's. "Lurking unseen. Forgotten."

"What do you mean?"

"Rosa tells me you think even the fire was deliberate, Danny. But we need evidence. Maybe you have a buried memory we could uncover. Something that fits with something else, that belongs together. Like jam and tea. Yes," Darko concludes, looking away into the dark heart of the Sagrada. "Jam 'n' tea . . ."

He taps the target with his knuckles.

"Do they go together?" Sing Sing says, baffled.

"Oh, yes. In eastern Europe. Black tea and a teaspoon of jam. Jam 'n' tea."

Darko frowns now. His eyes move quickly, tracking the flight of an unseen insect, fingers darting out and snipping at the air. There, its wings gripped between the tips of his thumb and forefinger, is a mosquito.

"Squash it. I hate mosquitoes," Sing Sing says.

"Most people do," Darko says, "but then again, they're just doing their own thing, aren't they? Just being mosquitoes, like knife throwers have to be knife throwers and escapologists have to be escapologists and clowns have to be clowns. All of us doing our best." He opens his fingers, and the insect whines away into the immense space around them.

"You're screwy," Sing Sing snorts. "Who doesn't kill mosquitoes?"

But Danny isn't listening. There's something familiar in what Darko says. A thought that he can't quite access. Something about shadows, something *in* the shadows. Stirring in the labyrinth . . .

Rosa's striding over quickly, her hand shielding her eyes from a powerful spotlight. Darko glances back at Danny and says quickly under his breath, "If the fire was deliberate, then I'd wager it was the same person who nixed the water cell, Danny. Gotta be."

"It's no good, she won't do it, Darko," Rosa says as she joins them. "Maria won't let you spin the wheel while you throw. And Izzy's not keen either—not after you nicked her in Milan."

Darko waves his hand, as if the matter is trivial. "That was a ricochet! We'll have to audition for Berl—"

But Danny's already turning to go, eager to slip away, to head for the Park.

"And where have you two been?" Rosa says, catching him by the arm. "I've been worried sick."

"Javier's dead," Sing Sing says abruptly. "Someone stabbed him with a flipping kitchen knife and now he's dead!"

Not what I wanted, Danny thinks. But it's a chance to see how Rosa and Darko react. Hardest for people to fake emotion when they're surprised with bad news. His eyes flick to Rosa, then Darko, then Rosa again. Their reactions are fast, but not *too* fast. They don't look rehearsed—just the sudden shock slapping them in the face, at the moment you'd expect it to hit. Natural enough.

"Whaaaaat?" Rosa shouts, eyes wide.

"Are you sure?" Darko says, slipping from the ball, as if shaken from it.

"There's a contract killer," Danny says, as calmly as he can manage. "She's out to get me. We think she killed Javier . . ."

"God in heaven!" Darko's voice stumbles.

"I don't know what's going on," Rosa says, "but I want you two really close. *Capiche*? Where's Zamora?"

"Telling Javier's wife the bad news," Danny says, his heart sinking. Now it's going to be really hard to get away to the Güell and start the hunt. He looks up at the building's crazy angles swaying over them. *Need to keep a clear head*, he thinks. That way at least whatever memory is stirring might come to the surface. He remembers that moment on Cheung Chau when he saw the Buddha statue—that supernaturally calm face, the fingers reaching down to touch the earth.

"What's your friend up to now?" Rosa moans.

Danny follows her gaze—and is alarmed to see that Sing Sing is stomping away toward the other members of the troupe, her shoulders set in determination.

"Sing Sing!" he shouts, hurrying after her, desperate to take back control, to get away to the park—out of this madhouse. *She'll go charging at things head-first, and we'll never get away. And it's MY story after all*, he thinks.

"Sing Sing!" he shouts again. But too late.

She's already in front of Aki, who's getting to his

feet, black Mohawk bristling under the spotlight, his chin raised defiantly.

"I want a word with you," Sing Sing says, shoving him, once, twice, three times in the chest and pushing the bemused Japanese flyer back against the wall.

He shoves her back. "What?"

"Got a flippin' question or two for you, Klown boy. You got any strange tattoos we don't know about? A lot of stupid dots, for example?!"

"What are you talking about?" he says.

Joey's on his feet now, color rising, stepping to his friend's defense. *Blast it*, Danny thinks. *It's going to end up in a real mess. What would Dad say . . . ?*

"You got a problem, Sing Song?" Joey snaps.

Bjorn, almost reluctantly, groans and raises himself from the floor, hands flexing ominously. Sing Sing turns from one to the other, the challenge thrown to each in turn.

"Come on then, losers!"

Danny runs to her side, the frustration mounting. She can take care of herself in a fight, he knows that, but there's no point getting everyone angry. Or injured.

"Can't you control your girlfriend, Danny-*chan*?" Aki says, pulling at Sing Sing's arm.

"I'm not his *flipping* girlfriend," Sing Sing shrieks, and quick as anything, she has his arm twisted up behind his back.

"Argh, *baka*!" Aki spits. "Stop!"

"Tell me what you know, or I'll break it worse than Zamora's," Sing Sing hisses, as she cranks the arm higher. Joey grabs at her, trying to break her hold, while Bjorn's eyes darken as he stalks over, struggling to control his temper.

"Get that stupid girl out of here!" he growls.

That's it. That's enough. "STOP IT!" Danny bellows.

His voice, suddenly loud, commanding, booms away in the echo chamber of the cathedral, bouncing off the stone pillars, taking control, taking center stage. As one, everybody stops still.

"Just STOP it! This isn't what the Mysterium's supposed to be. We're supposed to be a *company*! That means people working *together*! Dad would be furious to see this! Sing Sing, let Aki's arm go! Now!"

The girl does so, reluctantly, shoving Aki a half-push that nearly propels him off his feet.

"What's WRONG with everyone?!" Danny shouts. It feels like the spotlight is swiveling toward him, the magnetic focus of all eyes on him. *Keep going*, he thinks. *Dare to be a Daniel.*

"I don't care if you're pleased to see me or not— or if you wish I'd just go away or I'd *died* in the fire with Mum and Dad."

Silence in the great cathedral now. Just his voice, growing, gathering strength.

"I don't care what you think about me being here, but I do care that this company lives up to all the amazing things we've done in the past, that it lives up to the best of it. That we keep the heart and soul of the Mysterium intact. If anyone needs to tell me something—to clear the air—tell me NOW!"

Maria and the twins stand rooted to the spot. Darko is walking toward him with Rosa, both of them nodding in agreement. Up in the rigging Frankie is silently applauding. Billy sits on his amp, stroking his beard, eyes riveted on Danny, and Herzog comes trotting over, sitting down decisively right next to him, as if declaring his support at least. Danny's glad of that. He reaches down and ruffles the dog's head, but his eyes are still fierce, roving across the company members. There, he's said it— and everybody's listening for once. A kind of elation swells in his chest.

"Bravo!" Rosa says. "That's what I've been trying to say all along. You should all listen to this boy. Danny, you might not have an act for us, but you've got your dad's gift for firing this lot up."

There are murmured voices of agreement from all but Aki and Joey. They're still standing near Sing Sing, bodies angled in confrontation, tension in the upper chest, arms, shoulders. And Sing Sing still has her chin raised defiantly. She's not about to let things drop.

"These Klowns still have a lot of explaining to do, Danny. Particularly parrot-boy here. What was he doing talking to Jimmy T in Berlin?"

"You, missy, need to back off," Rosa says, shaking her head, her face whitening.

But Aki is staring at Sing Sing. "Who told you that?"

"Doesn't matter," Danny says, his voice still keeping its edge. "Somebody saw you talking to Jimmy."

Aki's eyes swing toward Rosa, as if willing her to speak. "Rosa can tell you I had nothing to do with it." He turns to Danny, exasperated. "I'm trying to help you! I want to help you with those codes. And I can tell you—on my honor—Jimmy had nothing to do with the fire. And neither did I."

With the fire, Danny notes. *He's not talking about the sabotage.* But they're getting closer, the moment of truth coming—

There's a heavy burst of radio static from the other side of the arena screen and a distorted voice crackling Spanish.

Danny swings around and sees two uniformed policemen standing in the opening of the stage curtain. A third man in plainclothes stands just behind them.

Their eyes are all trained on Danny.

28

WHY THE VAN SMELLED DODGY

Danny knows what it's about at once. He and Sing Sing must have been linked to the scene of Javier's murder. And maybe to the wreckage of the cable car. He wonders now if he should have chucked the matchbox—or the note he plucked from Javier's pocket. Or his own phone. *This might take hours and hours to explain, and we need to get to Park Güell.*

"Ugh, what now?' Rosa sighs, moving toward the men, but the older of the two police officers holds out his hand.

"*Señora.* We need to talk to the boy and girl here." He points to Danny and Sing Sing. "It will only take a couple of minutes or so."

"I'm in charge round here," Rosa says. "Talk to me."

"This is a criminal investigation. Into the death of *Señor* Javier Luis Toscano. These children may have been with him at the time—"

"But they had nothing to do with it," Darko says.

"They have failed to report a crime," the officer says, "and are suspected of tampering with a crime scene. We need to question them at the police station—"

"Then *I* want to be with them," Darko says, striding over. "And let me see some ID."

The officer flips out his badge and holds it for Darko to inspect. "You can wait outside the police station on Rossello Street. We have a liaison officer with us . . ." he points to the plainclothesman, "who will see that everything is OK."

Rosa beckons Danny and Sing Sing over. "It's OK. Just tell them what you saw."

Danny glances at the policemen. They're both tough, faces hardened on mean streets—and the light glints on the guns at their hips. The liaison man is slimmer, his shoulders hunched in a thick coat. He smiles encouragingly at Danny. "We need your help. For the victim's sake. His family."

"We aren't going anywhere," Sing Sing says defiantly.

"In that case," the first officer snaps, "you are being arrested."

The second officer steps forward, speaking rapidly in Spanish, reciting their rights as he takes a pair of handcuffs from his belt.

"But you can't cuff them," Rosa says, her voice raised.

"It is procedure," the older man says. "All arrests, we do this."

"It's OK," Danny says. "If it will help catch Javier's killer." He's thinking about the man's wife and two small children. How they beamed at their father just yesterday. How they're probably struggling to understand even now.

He holds out his wrists.

The young officer shakes his head, turns him around, and snaps the cuffs on tightly, pinning Danny's arms behind his back. The liaison officer steps forward and checks that the restraints are not too tight.

"Let me know if you are uncomfortable," he says, smiling again.

"You're not putting those things on me," Sing Sing snaps. "I want a lawyer."

"No point arguing," Danny says, resigning himself to the loss of time, of momentum. "Let's just get it done."

A white van is waiting outside the cathedral, and Danny and Sing Sing are ushered onto the bench seat. The younger officer gets in and sits down opposite them, and the door is slammed shut. He's drawn his pistol and rests it now on his lap.

"We'll follow," Rosa calls through the van window. "Don't worry."

Beyond her, Danny can make out Aki and Darko crossing the square, looking around for a taxi to hail, and then the van lurches away, banging off the curb, setting Danny and Sing Sing thumping against each other. Hard to steady yourself when your hands are tied behind your back.

"This can't be legal," Sing Sing mutters. "We're only kids."

The policeman opposite looks at her and shrugs.

"Hey, you! Do you speak English?"

"*Un poccito.*" Quickly he reaches up to grab hold of a strap hanging from the ceiling, bracing himself.

As if on cue, the van corners hard and then accelerates away up a side street, tires rumbling across the cobbles of a pedestrian zone, rattling over a speed bump. *Why the sudden urgency?* Danny thinks.

"What's going on?" he shouts over the roar of the engine.

The young policeman says nothing—but looks back through the rear window, checking the road behind him.

A heavy sensation of dread is taking hold of Danny. The van is unmarked—and it smells. The back is far from clean, with paper cups and fast-food cartons littering the floor. Danny's eyes switch back to the policeman.

"Who are you?"

The man ignores him.

"Where are you taking us?"

No response. The man shifts on his seat, bracing himself again as the van goes winging around another tight corner.

"We're in trouble, aren't we?" Sing Sing says, her voice tense, brittle.

"Yep."

"They're not real police officers, are they?"

"No."

Slowly, the man opposite picks up his gun, waving it casually in their direction. His eyes meet Danny's. "*Silencio.*"

Danny takes stock.

Not expecting trouble from the regular police, he took no precautions when the cuffs went on. They're snug against his skin, biting slightly, so no hope of slipping a wrist through them. The lock pick set is around his neck as always—and the universal key may well spring the cuffs—but how to get his hands free without this guy seeing him? How to get the gun away from him and stop the van, for that matter? Get the prep right for an escape and you're sailing, Dad used to say. Get it wrong and you're failing.

Now—unforgivably, he thinks—he's completely unprepared. Failing. Imbecile. No doubt where they're heading either. Special delivery to La Loca herself or maybe to some other part of the Forty-Nine. Then what?

In his mind he can't help seeing Rosa turning up the death card and seeing that black skeletal rider stalking the battlefield. Maybe this time the card means exactly what it says. But what will come first? Questioning? Torture of some kind?

Maybe, he thinks, *maybe we'll get a chance. Might just be one brief opportunity and we've got to be ready for it.*

Sing Sing has gone silent beside him, her shoulder jogging against his. *At least this time I have someone with me,* he thinks. *Someone who matters to me. I'm not alone. But I wish I hadn't dragged her into all this.*

He looks through the partition window into the cab. The older uniformed man is crouched over the wheel, elbows out, pushing the van hard as they head up a long drag, into the suburbs. The so-called liaison officer is on the passenger seat, a mobile against his ear, talking excitedly—but you can't hear anything over the moan of the engine, the rumble of the tires.

Danny scans the inside of the van. A flashlight lies on the floor—one of those powerful ones that Frankie always liked to use. Next to it, a couple of spades, some old and filthy blankets, a pickax. His heart stutters, missing its rhythm. *They're not off to dig something up, I'll bet. More a question of burying something. Someone.*

Us.

29

WHY IT'S GOOD TO HAVE A LONG LIFELINE

His spirit wavers, on the edge of surrender. So much to endure, so much effort to make. *Maybe I'm running out of reserves*, he thinks. *Maybe I should just give up and let things happen.* A fragment of a song rings in his head, something the Klowns sang against buzz-saw guitar. *Just wai . . . till fate . . . deals its mortal blowww . . .*

Sing Sing nudges his arm, turning her head toward him. There's still strength left in her, something vital and alive in the contact.

"Get his eyes," she hisses under his breath. "Get his attention, Danny." She's sliding down on the bench seat, acting out defeat, fear—even forcing tears to her eyes. But Danny can feel her body is wound tight, charged with contained energy.

"Please, *señor*," Danny says, sitting up, opening his eyes wider, trying to exaggerate the effect of the odd colors of the irises against the whites, knowing that in this gloom his pupils will be wide and deep.

The man looks back at him with vague interest—and Danny takes his chance. He opens his eyes a fraction farther and then goes for the hook. You focus on the surface of the subject's eyes, and then suddenly thrust your gaze deeper, as if reaching down the optic nerve itself, into the brain, right into the mind. Disconcerting if you nail it.

And he obviously *does* nail it, because the man's head snaps back, as if someone's jabbed him right in the eyes. He's blinking, shaking his head, a fish trying to wriggle off the hook.

That's all Sing Sing needs. Her right foot flies up without warning, a whiplash kick straight into the man's jaw. His head jerks violently back and bangs on the wall of the van. He slumps down.

Danny glances forward. They haven't heard up front. The van is rounding a corner, climbing up a steep side street, the foothills beyond Barcelona just visible as black silhouettes.

"My lock pick," he says. "Can you reach it if we go back-to-back?"

"I can do better than that," Sing Sing smiles. She sits on the rocking floor of the van, bringing her knees tight up to her chest, quickly working her bound hands down the back of her legs, under her feet.

"All that horrible contortionist training," she grunts, and suddenly she's standing back up again, steadying herself, her hands in front of her now.

"Excuse me." She reaches inside his T-shirt and pulls the pick from around his neck.

"It's in the recess on the back," Danny urges her. "Standard cuff lock key."

It's hard to hold steady as the van thumps through the backstreets, but at the third attempt Sing Sing gets the chubby key in the lock and Danny's cuffs spring loose.

She hands him the key, but at that moment they slam over a curb and he fumbles it.

"We haven't got long," Sing Sing hisses. "Get me free."

He drops to the floor, scrabbling for the key among the trash. It's come to rest next to the flashlight. Quickly he unlocks Sing Sing's hands, an idea taking shape. "Get ready."

"For what?"

"For anything."

He picks up the chunky flashlight, flicks the switch, and shines it against the palm of his hand. Just as he hoped: a powerful beam picking out the lines there, the long curve of his lifeline that Rosa once traced when he was a small boy. *A long, beautiful life, bello.*

Hope she's right about that!

Steadying himself with a deep breath, he clambers forward, waits for the van to take the next corner. And then with all the strength he can muster, he hammers on the partition window.

Startled, the driver and passenger look around as one. Danny's ready for that, the flashlight already trained at where he hopes the driver's eyes will be. And as the man swivels, he fires the dazzling beam. Direct hit!

The driver holds up a hand, looking away, blinded by the flashlight, hand flailing for the wheel, mouth open in panic. At this speed, in this tight knot of backstreets . . .

"Brace yourself!" Danny shouts and throws himself flat on the floor. The van jolts up onto the curb, wheels biting nothing for a moment, the engine churning. A loud bang as the front right bumper hits something, and then the whole vehicle flips up, catching another glancing blow and sending it keeling over onto its left side. Danny rolls with the movement, clutching the bench seat desperately with both hands, stopping himself from being thrown by the impact. A long screech of metal ripping the tarmac, another bang—and the van slides to a stop.

The safety glass between the front and backseat has blown, shattered by the force of the crash, but is still in place. Danny's already on his feet shining the flashlight to see what's happened to Sing Sing. She's in a tangle under the unconscious policeman but already wriggling free. There's a cut on her cheek, but otherwise, she looks OK.

"Now what?"

They both strain to listen. The men's voices are audible now, thick with shock and anger. Sounds like they're trying to open the passenger door, which is now pointing up at the night sky.

"Let's surprise them," she says, her eyes alight. "Let's attack!"

Before he can argue, she's taking a swift run up along the bench seat and kicking through the glass partition.

The fight is brief, claustrophobic, desperate.

As Danny clambers through the window, he finds Sing Sing grappling with the so-called liaison man, his arm and shoulder in a tight lock, the gun in his hand thrashing as he tries to aim and fire. The driver is slumped in the footwell, wedged among the pedals, trying to claw his way out, his legs bent at awkward-looking angles.

Danny aims the flashlight at him. The man's face is covered in blood, his nose pulped and broken. His shirtsleeve has been ripped, and as his forearm moves through the beam of light Danny sees the tattoo. It's the neat grid of dots, seven by seven. The circle on this one is closer to the center—second row out—and below it in red, the number 38.

Sing Sing's still locked in a clinch with the other man, and the gun goes off, horribly loud in the confined cab. Danny and Sing Sing both flinch, but it is the liaison man who howls in pain, looking down at where the bullet has torn into his thigh. He grimaces and pulls himself free of Sing Sing's grip, struggling to get his balance, to aim the gun again.

But the flashlight is still in Danny's hand. He brings it down with all his might onto the man's wrist, feeling the shudder as the heavy metal casing smacks the bone, breaking the man's grip. Sing Sing hisses an outbreath, chopping down hard on the high point of the man's shoulder. His eyes shut and he falls on top of the man struggling in the footwell.

Danny picks up the gun from where it has lodged on the dashboard and hurls it through the open passenger door.

"No escape," the driver groans. "We'll kill you like that dog Javier."

But Danny and Sing Sing are already climbing up out of the stricken vehicle, clambering onto its side. They drop to the street below. There's a smell of gasoline on the night air, and bits of engine are strewn across the pavement. A short way off, the battery lies broken in half, acid smoking in the streetlight.

Sing Sing's breathing hard, looking up and down the steeply sloping street. Some people farther down are shouting, running toward them.

"Let's just beat it," she says. "Any idea where we are?"

But Danny is already pointing at a sign fastened to the wall. "Maybe our luck's changing. At last."

He shines the flashlight at it, aware that as much as he's trying to keep his hand steady, the beam is shaking. *PARK GÜELL 500 meters*, the tourist sign reads. "This way to the memory palace."

Above their heads, the stars slowly emerge between the parting clouds, and in the distance, cresting the hills beyond Tibidabo, a full moon heaves into view.

30

WHY NO ONE IS CONSISTENT

By the time they reach the Park Güell, a silvery light is spilling across the city. In it, the park's squat, onion-domed gatehouses look like a stage set. Beyond, through heavy iron gates, steps lead up past a large lizard sculpture crouching in the moonlight. Danny stares at it now, feeling more memory awakening. He remembers the creature as multicolored and joyfully spouting water. Now it looks ghostly, its mouth dry, the checkered tiles bleached in the moonlight.

"So are we going in or not?" Sing Sing says.

She flashes him a smile, the blood smeared on her cheek. Even she's looking tired, more fragile than Danny's seen her before. And there's anxiety there too—as if she knows something's coming and she's got to face it, but she's not sure how it will go.

Frustrating that she won't tell me what it is, he thinks. *But I'm going to help her. Just like she's helping me.* He puts a hand on her arm. "Whatever happens, we keep together. From now on."

She nods quickly. "You bet."

With a quick look left and right, she puts a foot on the wall, reaches up for a handhold, and is up and over it before Danny has a chance to say more. He grabs hold of the rough wall, checks to see if anyone is watching. A security camera is panning their way. Can't be helped. Just one more thing to explain later, perhaps. If there *is* a later.

Right now the main thing is to keep moving. He jumps down to join her.

"We need to head up and to the left, I think," he says and starts up the stairway. "The mound must be over there, the highest part."

As he passes the lizard he thinks of himself—as a much younger boy—on a bright summer's day, not a care in the world, sitting astride the creature's back. It feels strange and sad. The same place, the very same point in space—but no overlap in time. No way to reach back.

Sing Sing's eyes are wide in the moonlight. "Any idea when your dad was last here?"

"Not for years, I think. But he was away a lot in those last few months. I thought he was doing stuff for other companies, but I guess it was the work for Interpol."

"So you don't really know where he was. Or what he was doing?"

"No."

It feels devastating to admit this—that someone so close, so important, who shaped you so much—could have a life so hidden from you, so unknown.

"It seems to me," Sing Sing says, picking her words carefully, "it seems he expected people to be honest and open with him. But not always the other way around."

Danny sighs. "Only the dead are consistent."

"What?"

"Something he used to say."

"Handy!"

The darkness thickens as they come to the top of the stairs. Ahead, a forest of stone pillars holds up a wide, flat roof, like some kind of Egyptian temple. The moonlight picks out the first few, and the rest fade into black beyond. *Is this where I played hide-and-seek with Mum and Zamora?* he wonders. *It could be.*

"We go up to the side of it."

Another flight of steps curves up to the right of the pillared hall and takes them up onto its roof.

Sing Sing whistles softly.

A vast square lies before them, the gravel gleaming in the fullness of the moon. To their left, it runs away to a wavelike balcony lined with tiled benches. Beyond, looking back over the park gates, the city is a stunning panorama, picked out in monochrome, a black-and-white version of the familiar cityscape. The only color comes from the red lights dotted on top of the Sagrada cranes, some distant neon toward Plaça de Catalunya. Beyond that, the blankness of the sea.

"I bet this was one of the memory points," Danny says. But whatever was patterned in Dad's neurons and synapses might just as well never have existed. The fire obliterated everything—flesh and bones and memories and fears and hopes. Everything you saw and tried to capture and understand. *You gather stuff all your life*, Danny thinks, *and then it just falls apart when you die. Disappears.*

But not quite. That photograph of Javier's comes

back to him. Mum and Dad—just visible—ghost faces in the darkened mirror, frozen in time. The mystery of it all, surrounding him . . .

A smile of understanding creeps across his face. Of course!

Behind them, the hillside is wreathed in shadow, just the agitated tops of the palm and pine trees lit, shifting in the breeze.

"Mystery!" he says out loud.

"What?" Sing Sing says, baffled.

"Mysterium. It's the answer to the second clue. The Latin for mystery is *Mysterium*. It's all around us all the time. That's the keyword to the second code, of course."

"Then let's crack it now," Sing Sing says eagerly.

"No. We'd better keep moving. Maybe the Forty-Nine know where we are. That guy who pretended to be a policeman must have been the sector head, but there could be more. And La Loca's still out there."

They turn from the view, making their way hurriedly past stacked café tables and chairs, folded parasols. A hush lies over the park, and every sound comes at them loudly: parakeets rustling in the trees, the sound of their own feet on the gravel. The place is designed for pleasure, to be thronged with people. Empty and dark, it feels sinister, threatening, every shadow a likely place of ambush or attack.

A path snakes up between the foliage, skirting battered, graffiti-covered cactus, trees shutting down for winter. They climb steadily in silence, senses straining, past formal areas and then on into a knot of woodland, the earth and pine needles soft underfoot, gaining height all the time.

Danny comes to a stop, lifting his hand, listening intently. He turns to look behind them, back through the twisty pines, the splashed patches of moonlight.

"Someone's following us."

"You sure?"

He listens again. Nothing but his own heartbeat to be heard now. "I thought I heard footsteps—and when we stop, they stop. But just a tiny bit later."

They both strain, listening for the space between their own breath, the sigh of the wind.

"Maybe it was just our echo?" Sing Sing says, shutting her eyes to concentrate.

"Maybe. We won't hear whoever it is on this soft ground anyway."

They move on, their shoes kicking up leaf mulch and rust-colored needles and earth. And then the trees open onto a moonlit playground. A basketball hoop stands sentinel in the clearing beside some swings, a roundabout.

Danny glances around. "Let's get across fast and then wait."

Together they sprint across the open ground, tense, expectant, feet kicking up gravel. It sounds very loud in the stillness of the park.

As they drop into bushes on the far side, Danny looks back. Is that a shadow moving? There! Just beyond the silhouetted swings. A figure that moved, then stopped?

"Do you see it?" he whispers.

"I think so."

Danny holds his breath.

Yes! Moving again, coming forward, hesitantly, into the moonlight. Shoulders hunched, tense.

And then Danny sees the thick, short Mohawk. The glint of a piercing as the figure turns its head.

Aki.

31

WHY CACTI CAN
BE USEFUL

The Klown comes a step or two farther onto the playground, looking briefly in their direction and then away again.

"Whaaat's he doing here?" Sing Sing whispers. Danny holds a finger to his lips, keeping his eyes glued to the Klown. Aki seems unsure of what to do, turning first one way and then another, before pulling a folded piece of paper from his pocket, holding it up to the moonlight. He turns it the other way up, hesitates again, and then moves quickly off to the right, away from them.

"So we were right about him," Sing Sing growls. "Scumbag."

"We can't be sure," Danny says. That uncertainty

in Aki's movements doesn't suggest aggression. More like confusion, like he's sniffing something out too. "Let's find this hill as quickly as we can."

"He'll be sorry if he crosses my path," Sing Sing says, cracking the knuckles of her right hand.

But Danny is already on his way again, hurrying, memory guiding his feet through the dance of shadows in the woods. Excitement building.

Yes, it's this way, I remember it. A kind of mound. Curled like a snail. You put your mind, your memory, in a place, and it starts to unwind, starts to come back up into consciousness. Just like Dad said, it's all crouching down there, in that dark maze of the memory, waiting to come back to the light. If you're brave enough.

Something else is stirring, something to do with what Darko said. Things lurking in the shadows.

Things that belong together.

And then, in a flash of perfect recall, he sees what his mind has been struggling to grasp. As if a video file has been buffering for ages and suddenly there's enough bandwidth and it's playing right in front of his eyes.

It's the night of the fire. The flames are at their worst, the snow is thick and getting thicker—and

Danny's looking around, from one member of the company to the other, hoping, willing someone to do something.

But everyone's already done what they can, and the fire extinguishers lie spent on the ground and they're all giving up, backing away from the searing intensity of the fire, choking from the effects of the smoke. Darko calling the emergency services yet again, Frankie and Izzy fumbling to connect a hose to a frozen tap.

Danny starts to run toward the flames, but Zamora grabs hold of him.

And he looks around to see if *anything* else can be done. And there in the shadows is a dark shape.

A man in a flap-eared trapper cap, standing watching, the light of the fire not quite reaching him—and then he's turning and very slowly, very deliberately walking away from the tragic scene, not coming to help, not rushing to look for the fire crews, just plodding away into the darkness and the thickening snowflakes until he is gone. Forgotten.

Until now.

Surely that's the person who's responsible for the fire then! Watching the results and then vanishing. Everyone else was accounted for, staring in horrified fascination at the intensity of the fire, the sizzling snow. All the Klowns, all the Aerialisques, Darko, Rosa, Zamora, Frankie, Billy, Herzog . . .

This silhouetted figure is the one.

"What? What's the matter?" Sing Sing's looking at him anxiously. "Did you see old wacky-Aki again?"

In the grip of the recall—the revelation of the mystery figure—he's almost forgotten his friend, let alone the wandering Klown.

"No," he says. "No."

Danny shuts his eyes, fighting to hold the image, to resolve the face under that snow-laden cap as it turns back to the darkness.

Jimmy T, surely! The face floats in his mind's eye, quite clearly. The lines that would crease even deeper when he laughed or swore. The hooded eyes he made up to such effect for his Doctor Oblivion routine.

"Come on, Danny, let's find this hill. Before someone finds us."

Danny opens his eyes. His heart's beating wildly now, elation and adrenaline charging his body.

"What is it?!"

"I'll tell you later. Let's go."

Renewed determination, renewed confidence drive Danny as he cuts through the trees, pulled steadily and surely through the park. *You go around here, through this knot of trees . . .*

It's like going deeper into Dad's labyrinth, following the trail left for him. And now Danny's memory is awake, alert, as if his feet remember the path through the park, closing in on the goal.

And there it is!

Standing on the flattened brow of a hill is a conical mound. It's faced with stones, a twisting path leading to its top, the whole thing dramatically lit by the moon that's now hanging high overhead.

Danny races forward to the bottom of the path, then clambers up, two steps at a time, lifted up onto the highest point of the Güell, with all of the city arrayed below him to the south, and six or seven low hills encircling the other sides. A silver path glitters on the dark sea pointing toward them.

"This is it. This is the memory point. The last place," he calls out, forgetting for a moment the need for stealth and silence.

Sing Sing joins him on the top, panting hard. "And now what?"

His spirits stumble at that simple question. "I don't know. Start looking for something."

What did I expect to find? he thinks. *A flashing sign? Somebody waiting to show me what to do? If Dad put something here, he'll have hidden it well, but he'll have left a mark of some kind, a pointer.*

But what?

"Spread out," Danny says desperately. "There must be something obvious."

He flicks the flashlight into life. "I'll take the side in shadow."

But five minutes' intense search fails to produce anything other than random bits of graffiti, initials and dates, names that mean nothing to them. No symbol or word that slaps you in the face. No *H.W.* for Harry White. No *D.W.* for Danny Woo. No *Mysterium* or even *X marks the spot.*

The mound's near the back wall of the park. Now and then a car swishes by on a road behind a service gate—and they stop and listen and wait for it to go, just in case. Danny's excitement has given way to a kind of nervy restlessness now. *Maybe we misread the clue*, he thinks.

"I can't see anything," Sing Sing calls. Her voice is dejected too. "But there must be something here.

There *must* be. Maybe we should take a look at that second code."

She walks away from the mound and slumps on a bench. Behind her a clump of cactus crouches, the wide, flat leaves like bright hands in the moonshine.

"And what made you go all weird in the woods? Looked like you'd seen a flipping ghost."

"I'll tell you in a minute."

He clambers down from his perch on the side of the mound, pulling the ever-more-creased sheets of paper from his pocket.

"It might take ages to crack this. We still don't know where the keyword goes on the top row."

There's a sound now.

A distinct movement in the bushes behind Sing Sing. Danny flicks on the flashlight, playing it across the cactus, into the shadows. Nothing to see but the contorted trees, their foliage burning with the change of the season, and the cactus, their leaves gouged with more graffiti, initials and years and hearts and . . .

And then he sees his own name. Cut neatly into a broad cactus leaf is the word *DANNY*. Not as white as some more recent initials and words, but not as browned and blurred as older stuff. And under it is that infinity symbol smoothly looping through its double knot—just like Dad used to leave for Mum! Below that is the number 15.

Danny rushes past Sing Sing, bends to the graffiti and puts his finger to the letter *D*. Even cut in a cactus the writing is familiar, forceful. Dad! He was here and cut this—no doubt. And the 15? *Must be fifteen paces from here, that's the obvious thing . . .*

He stands with his back to the plant, and taking exaggerated strides, trying to match Dad's paces, he counts one, two, three—past the bench and the watching figure of Sing Sing, across the gravel—seven, eight, nine—up to the base of the mound—twelve, thirteen, fourteen. His foot touches the sloping rock wall. One more pace would be about halfway up, so he climbs, flashlight held between his teeth, checking each stone carefully.

Must be about here, surely. He takes the flashlight and plays it desperately across the rocks and sees, etched into one of them, a small exclamation mark. Surprise! It seems to say.

"Sing Sing! Come here," he calls under his breath. He grips the rock with his fingertips and tries to pull it away, but it's held tight, snagged by small stones and dirt. There's just a slight movement.

"Get me a stick or something! Quick!"

He digs his nails down the side of the stone, pulling back gravel and soil as best he can while Sing Sing scrambles up to join him.

"Try this." She hands him a snapped-off piece of pine, strong enough and with a little kink to the end. Quickly he works it into the crack, raking back the dirt and grit, trying to free up the rock. Suddenly the stick sinks much deeper into the crevice.

"It's hollow behind! Hold the flashlight for me!"

The strong beam cuts into the mound, and there, bright yellow, is a folded plastic bag.

Two more minutes of frantic digging, and Danny's excavated more of the improvised mortar used to jam the stone in place. Working the stone again with his fingers, it suddenly comes loose, falling down to the ground, nearly braining Sing Sing as it goes.

He reaches into the coolness of the recess and pulls the bag out, his fingers trembling now, eager, hopeful, the suspense making him feel clumsy—not wanting Sing Sing to see the shake in his hands.

"You take the torch."

Unfolding the package confirms what he thought: the distinctive logo and color of a bag from

El Ingenio. Of course that's what Dad would use! The contents rustle in the plastic. About a pound in weight.

"Open it! Open it, Danny!"

He blows out through pursed lips, like someone blowing on hot food, calming himself—and then reaches inside.

Past and present collapsing into each other . . .

A book. And an envelope.

He pulls them out into the glare of the torch beam. For a moment the book means nothing to him: it's a well-thumbed paperback with the words *MARCEL PROUST* in large red letters and the title *In Search of Lost Time Volume I*. He's disappointed. Baffled, in fact. It's like opening a Christmas present meant for someone else, makes no sense at all. But a piece of paper is sticking out just above the cover, and he pulls it out to see Dad's writing again. That's better!

Speaking to him, as if standing at his shoulder, the tone loud even in the writing.

This is important, old son!!!

"What's the book?" Sing Sing says, her voice betraying disappointment.

But Danny ignores her. Written hastily on the thick manila envelope there's more from Dad:

Danny. If you are reading this, then the worst may have happened and I'm no longer around. Things are looking a bit dicey right now, but maybe Mum can explain if I can't. Knew you'd find this all right. No doubts about your abilities! I wonder when you're opening this. I wonder how tall you are, how old you are. I wonder what led you here—what you want to ask me? One thing you WILL want to know is contained within. Do your best with it—you ought to know. And I hope you know that we love you.

Dad X

Danny swallows hard. And again, his eyes fill.

"What's in the flipping envelope?" Sing Sing chirps. "Let me see!"

Danny shakes away the emotion, biting hard on his lip as he pulls the contents from the stiffened envelope and the moonlight flickers across it.

A single sheet of thick paper. Stamped with a crest and the words: *Hong Kong Municipal Council: Birth Certificate.*

It's filled out in black ink—a mixture of Chinese characters and English.

Before he can stop her Sing Sing snatches it from him, shining the torch onto it, her eyes darting across the paper.

Against the word *MOTHER*, the English writing reads *WOO, LILY.* Next to *FATHER*, the single word *UNKNOWN*.

And against *CHILD'S NAME*, the words *SING SING*.

Danny's mouth drops open.

Sing Sing's face is lit from below with the reflection of the flashlight off the glossy paper, her own eyes wide, her own mouth open as she stares at the words.

"I knew it! I knew it! I flipping well knew it!"

She sits down heavily on the dusty ground and bursts into tears.

32

WHY THE CLOWN SQUEALED

The moon sails higher, lighting the ragged edges of the clouds, the watching cactus, the two small figures sitting huddled on the ground.

"So why did she abandon me then?!" Sing Sing wails, as the sobbing shakes through her chest and shoulders. She's sitting on the bench, struggling for breath, the paper clutched in her hands.

Gingerly Danny takes it from her grasp, anxious that she will crumple it up—by accident or in anger—and keen to read the words again for himself.

It's as if the world has suddenly got that much larger, that much more bizarro—its volume cranked up, roaring long-kept secrets right into his ears. Dad's words still ringing—and emotion flooding with them—but this is more disorientating by far. The official words on the birth certificate stare back at him.

Mother: Lily Woo.

Child's name: Sing Sing.

Weight: 3.9 kgs.

Father: Unknown.

Mother's occupation: Performer . . .

Date of birth: February 23rd.

A sister, he thinks, shaking his head in disbelief. *I've got a sister—or half of one at any rate.* And, strangely enough, it makes sense. *She said she was looking for her mother. She feels so like me—*

"You're a Pisces," he mutters.

"Huh?"

"February 23rd is Pisces. Rosa always says Pisceans make the best wire walkers. Blondin and a whole bunch of the others . . ."

He sits down on the bench and puts an arm on her sloping shoulders. It feels easier somehow to calm Sing Sing's distress than deal with his own bewilderment.

"But you said your mum died a long time ago, when you were little."

"That's what I was told. That's what I believed

for years. I didn't know any more than that she'd died when I was young, that my father was a bad guy who died before I was even born."

"Then what?"

"I grew up with Charlie. Learned some kung fu. Got bored with that and took up acrobat stuff, learned to walk a slack wire. Then I got interested in the circus and got digging around on the Internet. Then one day I found the Mysterium website, and I took one look at Lily and I knew—I just *knew*—that she was my mother. No idea how. And I started to dig and dig—and then I got lucky. I met Ricard through Chow—and the rest is history."

"And what about your father?"

"His name was Anthony Leung. As far as I can tell, he died just like they said. He was up to his neck in triad crap."

She breathes deeply, then vigorously wipes the tears away. "So here I am. Your abandoned, orphaned half sister. Don't know why I don't feel happier."

Danny nods, his excitement now held in check by the knowledge that Mum could have been so heartless as to abandon her own child.

"She must have had her reasons," he says, trying to convince himself as much as Sing Sing.

"Did she ever say anything about me?"

"No. I'm sorry. But I overheard an argument or two . . ."

His voice trails off. *We all have our baggage, Lily. You must know that! Better than anyone*, Dad had snapped.

And Mum had looked as though he had hurt her, deeply, right to the very core.

"We're together now, though, right?" Danny looks into her eyes.

She looks back, summoning strength, taking deep breaths to fight away the tears. "You bet, Danny Woo. Every step of the way—"

The scrunch of gravel underfoot makes them both jump—and they look up to see Aki gazing down at them, his mohawk jet black against the moon beyond, face shadowed.

"Romantic stroll?" he drawls. "Don't want to interrupt."

Sing Sing lets out a growl of rage. All the withheld frustration pulsing through her system, she leaps tigerlike from the bench, arms out, fingers splayed, taking the surprised Aki down in one flying tackle, then pinning him to the ground, pushing her face into his.

"I'm going to mush you, Klown," she hisses. "What are you doing, following us?"

"I'm—I'm just trying to help," he says, winded by the fall, struggling to free his hands. "Rosa sent me. I followed the police van on a scooter—and then I heard the crash. Somebody said you went toward the Güell and I caught sight of you on that big square— and then I lost you—"

"Bull!"

"It's the truth."

Danny crouches down beside Aki. "Sing Sing will let go if you just answer me one question."

Aki winces as Sing Sing pushes down with her knee into his stomach. "OK. OK."

"What were you doing with Jimmy T that night in Berlin?"

"Nothing."

"Don't lie to me, Klown," Sing Sing snarls. "Don't make me mad!" She inches her knee lower.

"OK! Argh. I'll tell you. I did see him. I saw Jimmy. But I was just a messenger."

"Who for?" Danny barks.

"Not saying."

"You've got three *flipping* seconds. I know how to hurt you."

"OK. OK." Aki shuts his eyes tight. "For Rosa. She had seen him hanging around, and she wanted me to warn him off. In case he did anything stupid. But he didn't listen. It was Jimmy who sabotaged the water torture cell. I'm sure of it."

Danny pats Sing Sing on the back then, relief and triumph surging through him. Aki's evidence matches the recovered memory of Jimmy in the snow. *We're going to get to the bottom of this at last!*

"He's telling the truth, Sing Sing," he says. "Rosa was stashing something away in the prop store— maybe something to do with the sabotage."

"I don't buy it!" Sing Sing says. "He's lying."

Danny shakes his head. "I have an eyewitness who can put Jimmy T at the scene—"

"But that's impossible," Aki says, sitting up as Sing Sing releases him. "Jimmy was back in America by then. Rosa's sure he had nothing to do with the fire. Absolutely 100 percent sure."

"I need to talk to Rosa," Danny says, picking up the Proust book and the envelope from the bench. "She held things back from me—from Dad too. Maybe . . ." He can't voice the thought—that if Rosa had spoken up, Mum and Dad would still be alive.

"Here, put them in this," Sing Sing says, holding open the yellow bag. "And let's get back to the Mysterium."

They make their way down through the park.

Clouds are blowing in from the sea again, obscuring the moon for minutes at a time. It's darker in the thickly planted parts of the Güell, but the way down seems easier than the way up. *After all*, Danny thinks, *I'm carrying treasure back from the hill. A message from Dad, a sister, more evidence . . . Maybe the worst is over.*

An uneasy truce hangs between Aki and Sing Sing, and all three of them are shut up tight inside their own thoughts.

Danny steals a glance at Sing Sing, new questions pushing through his mind. Why on earth was it all kept so secret? Why did Mum abandon her young baby all those years ago? If Dad knew he was in trouble, why hide this package in his memory palace? *Why not just tell me about Sing Sing, tell me what was going on?* You answer one question and three spring up. Like trying to cut the heads off a Hydra.

The birth certificate makes a kind of sense. And the note—that's somehow both more and less than he hoped to find here. *Dad reaching out to me again, but not telling me enough. Like always. Leaving you hanging for more. And what's the Proust book doing there? He said it's important, so it must be,* Danny thinks, ransacking his memory.

Dad was obsessed with the book that last year. Evening after evening he sat tucked up on the bench seat, frowning, squinting, sometimes reading bits out loud, sometimes looking baffled, once hurling it in frustration across the caravan. The book and Dad's battle with it became a standing joke. But why wall it up here?

"You and your bloody Proust," Mum complained one day, when she felt she was doing more than her fair share of work and Dad had been sunk in the book for several days.

"Mmm. Bloody Proust," Dad said distantly.

Danny had peered at the dense pages of text. "What's it about?"

"It's just a man remembering his life. He dunks a biscuit—a little cake thing really—in his tea and eats it, and in that moment he remembers his entire childhood, his life. Growing up, family, all that. It's kind of about nothing. And everything."

"You're just trying to act intellectual on us, Harry," Mum had snorted. "Competing with Laura!" And a spiky exchange had followed, which ended up with Dad stomping out of the trailer and banging the door shut behind him.

Why leave the book for me? Surely a thousand-page story about a man eating a biscuit and remembering his childhood can't help me now, Danny thinks, exasperated.

Aki is trotting along beside Danny and Sing Sing, looking from one preoccupied face to the other.

"Are you both OK?" he says.

"I don't know anymore," Danny says. "How about you—sister?"

Sing Sing manages a half-smile. "I don't flipping know either. Brother!"

"I could help," Aki starts to say. "I could help you with those codes, Danny. I mean if—"

But he doesn't get out another word.

A dull thud echoes across the park as the baseball bat slams into his head, felling him with a sickening blow, laying him out cold on his back, the blood bright on his face.

Simultaneously Danny feels a pair of strong hands reach around his neck and mouth. Really strong.

And a voice sings in his ear. "Time for bed," and then something soft is being pressed to his mouth, gagging him, filling his nose and throat, clouding his head in a rush that seems to drown out every thought . . .

And the last thing he sees is Sing Sing, fighting desperately for her life, parrying, blocking, falling as two men in hoodies kick and punch her to the ground.

"Sleep tight," the voice whispers in his ear. "Sleep tight for La Locaaaaaaaaa."

He falls.

Falls into an abyss of swirling sounds and lights, spiraling down, and knows nothing more but the sensation of falling.

33

WHY ROSA WAS RIGHT

It's not sleep but something longer, deeper, more troubling. Restless and full of movement and effort. It leaves him feeling nauseous to the pit of his stomach, struggling for air, trying hard to release the pressure on his chest, the thudding ache in his head.

He's bound tight in what feels like the rigid embrace of a night terror—awake and yet dreaming so all the muscles are paralyzed and a terrible sense of dread is adding more weight to his chest, his shoulders.

Death coming. The skeletal horseman . . .

Breathe! he thinks. Breathe and wait for it to subside like they always do—and the sinister figure looming over your bed turns out to be no more than the coat you hung on the wardrobe door, black witch or gray-eyed alien shrinking, evaporating.

He feels the breath struggling in his chest. The sense of restriction, of immobility doesn't shift. Hard to move at all.

Are my eyes open or not? I'm opening them—but I can't see anything. Or is that a chink of light? So thirsty, mouth's so dry, like he hasn't had a drink for days.

The blood is heavy in his head, singing in his ears. *Can't move my feet or legs.*

He struggles to move again. What is going on?

And then he hears it. An unmistakable sound. Something that he heard from the very first day he was born—that probably he heard in the womb.

The sound of countless childhood days—as unmistakable as the sound of Frankie rigging a show or Rosa singing dirty songs on her caravan steps in the morning or Herzog barking or Mum laughing . . .

He hears the sound of an excitable and expectant Mysterium audience. A packed house waiting to see what is about to happen, intrigued by the rigging, the steampunky props, the sight of the Aerialisques ascending to the very highest part of the hemisphere. *The show is about to start*, he thinks, still confused, still struggling for understanding. *The show's about to start and I'm about to miss it.*

Something weird, though: it sounds like the audience hum is coming from somewhere above his head . . .

If I could just wake up. Head so heavy, like it's going to burst.

Then a new sound: the looping drone of Billy starting the intro music for part two of the Wonder Chamber show. The guitar fills his ears and the crowd starts to whoop and applaud, but everything seems wrong. They're up in the air above him.

And then, as the last muffling effects of the drug wear off, the realization dawns.

I'm upside down! Hanging by my ankles.

As he struggles, he can now feel the sway and movement of the rope or whatever it is that is suspending him.

So why can't I see? Free my arms?

But he already knows. The music below stumbles a beat and then cuts out entirely—and a gasp wells up from the people far below.

Even before he smells the pungent, choking aroma of the burning paraffin, he knows what's happening.

I'm the Hanged Man!

34

WHY THE CIRCUS ALWAYS HAS TO GO ON

Zamora is only half-watching as the second part of the show kicks into life. Tiredness, anxiety, and the side effects of strong painkillers are all taking their toll.

He has argued with Rosa to postpone the opening night—to concentrate all their efforts on finding Danny, on helping the police—but the ringmistress has told him it's impossible, that they will be ruined financially and have nothing left, that they must carry on and hope for the best. "*Viva il circo,*" she growled. "Whatever happens."

And, through furious tears, he knew she was right. A capacity crowd was expected, and there was nothing else to be done but somehow put on a brave face and do what they were all born to do. Perform.

Now behind heavy eyes, Zamora is replaying the events of the last twenty or so hours.

He and Sing Sing and Aki and Frankie kept searching long after the others returned exhausted and silent from combing the Güell. Together they kept going all night, all the following morning, out into the streets of El Raval and the Gothic Quarter and the Eixample.

The police have thrown all their resources at the missing boy, the description of the woman is with every officer and patrol in the city, and the ports and airports are alerted—but not a trace has been found.

Sing Sing stands now quietly beside Zamora, watching Billy climb to his guitar platform. Her face is white, drained of energy, scuffed and bruised from her fight with the men in hoodies. It was only as she kicked the second one over the parapet that she could turn to help Danny—and by then he and the Loca woman were nowhere to be seen.

Aki lay sparked out in the gravel and took ten minutes to come around.

Despite seeing double, the Klown refused to go to the hospital and joined the search with as much determination as Zamora or Sing Sing. Now he's sitting on the bench in the curtain, stretching, adjusting the bandage wrapped around his forehead.

"I should have got back from Lope's quicker," Zamora mutters to himself.

Sing Sing shakes her head. "I shoulda kept my flipping eyes open."

"If wishes were fishes . . ." Zamora starts to say.

And then he's aware that all the eyes of the crowd are swiveling up, way up over the top of the rigging, past where Izzy and Beatrice and Maria are tying on their safety lines, preparing for the black angels routine. Way up into the somber darkness above—where a flickering light has suddenly kindled into life.

Shouldn't be anything there, he thinks. *What's going on now?* He walks forward, shielding his eyes to ward off a spotlight, peering into the gloom.

"What's going on?"

Rosa is standing nearby, dressed in her full ring-mistress glory, roses threaded through her hair, pointing up toward the distant, vaulted ceiling.

"Frankie! Aim a spotlight up there!" she shouts.

There's flame curling high under the roof of the cathedral now, licking its way up a long rope, throwing unearthly shadows onto the pillars around it . . .

And Frankie's light illuminates a black sack, spinning, jiggling, shaking, dancing a crazy, desperate dance under the hungry flames eating their way through the rope.

A gasp now from the crowd as the black shape falls, sailing down toward the floor a hundred feet below, a sack falling away from the burning rope, revealing a small figure, bound tight in a straightjacket, ankles shackled together. Fighting to free itself as the flames burn closer.

In the sudden silence that fills the arena you can hear the flames sighing high above—and then Sing Sing's voice, bright, fragile.

"Danny!"

Zamora is already on the move, rushing for the spiral staircase nearby. Darko following close behind.

Maybe I can do something if I can get up there, Zamora thinks. But in his heart of hearts, he knows that rope's almost toast.

35

WHY DANNY DID THE DEATH DANCE

As soon as Danny smells the paraffin—that pungent aroma that scented so many childhood evenings—he realizes what's happening.

It's the burning rope escape.

"The rope's a real killer," Dad always said. "Seen a man die that way myself. But fine as long as you know what you're doing . . ." he would add, seeing alarm on Danny's young face.

Fine if you know what you're doing.

He has no idea how he has ended up here—only remembers La Loca's dreadful grip and the stink of whatever was on the handkerchief that she used to gag his mouth and nose—but he knows exactly what he's up against.

Even as he fights to shake the bag from him, he can feel the tight bind of the straightjacket, his arms crossed over his chest and fastened behind his back where the straps are wrenched to maximum tightness. The restraints at his ankles are normally locked to the figure-eight coupling that takes the rope loop. *Are there chains too? Don't think so.*

How long has he been hanging there? How long until the flames bite through the rope? A synthetic hemp will take longer than a natural one to give—but it depends on the amount of fuel—how long it's already been flaming. Too many variables to work it out.

So he starts to fight, every single muscle in his body, expanding, contracting, twisting—desperate for any piece of slack.

And now the bag is loose and gone—and he's blinking in the lights, and the floor seems a horribly long way away. No chance of surviving that fall.

A thousand or more faces are staring up at him, little circles of awed attention, fixed on his struggle. Do they know it's for real, or do they think it's part of the show? He can see the Aerialisques positioned halfway between him and the ground, can hear people calling his name, can see the upthrust of the

Sagrada's pillars and staircases all around, the glowing, flickering lights that spell out the one word: *MYSTERIUM*.

Forget that. Look up—see what's to be done.

He cranes his head forward, looking up toward his feet, past the straps of the straightjacket to the leather cuffs holding his ankles. It's Dad's own equipment, he realizes.

The flames are pluming bright and hot. Just a couple of arms' lengths away, chugging black smoke to the ceiling above. *Can't see through that, can't see how I'm fixed or to what.* At least the flames are a definite orange, not bright yellow—or white—which means it's a cool flame. One of the fuels Frankie uses for effect.

Still time to free myself, he thinks. *But then what?!* He feels the movement of the lock pick set around his neck, working its way up under his sweatshirt, tugged by gravity around his blood-filled head. *But no good until I've got my arms free.*

So go for it, he thinks. *One thing, then another . . .* He sets himself going in Dad's "death dance." The shimmying, jerking jig that will set him twisting on the rope, send him spinning—that will buy some slack. But that will also put strain on the weakening rope. Arms straining, heart pounding, vision blurring.

The fire, the drop into the abyss, the straight-jacket. Nothing else. Try and forget you're putting more stress on that steadily thinning cord that's keeping you alive.

And then he can feel the give he needs—just enough, *just* enough to start to work his arms up his chest, still wriggling, still twisting—the sinews in his shoulders starting to scream in complaint, hot with the effort of the muscles, the wrenching of the shoulder close to dislocation, everything telling him to stop for fear of damaging his own body.

Ignore it. Push hard now.

Arrrgh. Pain shoots through both shoulder sockets—but then he's done it. Arms up, the straps behind his back freed, over his head. No chains, at least. Just the buckles and straps of the jacket. Quickly he starts to work them loose, fiddling the leather through the buckles. Hard when you're spinning like crazy.

There are screams from below. But cheers too. The crowd's confused.

But now, disaster.

In one violent movement he feels the bootlace holding the lock pick slip over his head. It snags briefly on an ear and then slides off and is gone. He watches it fall into space, heart sinking.

Danny looks up again to the flames—very close now. And the rope's giving little shudders, telltale signs that it's losing fibers, losing strength. But he can see something else. No master lock on the leather shackles! Just the heavy straps.

Whoever did this didn't know exactly what they were doing. Or were they giving him a chance? Either way it's good news.

He pulls himself up, abdominal muscles straining, hands reaching for his ankles, eyes bright with stars as the blood shifts. Shakes his head to clear his vision and then goes about forcing the buckles loose on the restraint.

They're going, going! Then what?!

That's it—you reach up and take the weight on the figure-eight link with your hand. And then when you're hanging free by your hands, they lower you to the ground.

But no one's going to do that now.

He looks around frantically, hearing a snap in the fiber of the rope above. About fifteen feet away there's a balcony—one of the high ones tight under the Sagrada's roof. It's the only chance.

Quickly he does what he saw Dad do so many times. The last triumphant releasing thrust of the hand to the foot shackles—and then he's hanging by his arms from the link fastened onto the eye of the rope, the restraint falling to the ground far below. More of the crowd cheering now!

But no time to dwell on that. Just the hitch and kick of his legs, setting the rope swinging—first just a little sway—but then amplifying the motion, the arc getting bigger and bigger and bigger. Long, looping swings that take him closer and closer to the stone balcony.

One attempt only. No safety net. No harness. No room for error.

Here I go.

At least if I go, I go like Wallenda.

Two more . . . one . . . now!

He lets go of the metal link at the end of the swing and for a moment is flying, a great whoosh of air in his ears, arms out to stabilize his fall, and then *whump*, he's down, knees compressing to absorb the shock, landing hard on the balcony, stumbling just one long step and then he's dropping to his knees, the force of the landing, the long minutes spent upside down, the fear all taking their toll. He looks back through the bars of the balcony.

The rope is still burning brightly, dancing like mad now that it's lost the burden of his weight. Now it snaps, and—a fiery comet—goes arching down into the nave below, trailing smoke and sparks.

And now the cheering starts.

36

WHY THE PARAKEETS SCREECHED IN THE NIGHT

Danny doesn't wait another moment. He ducks through a small doorway and finds himself on one of the twisting staircases. Footsteps below—coming this way. Someone coming to help? He starts down the first spiral . . .

From somewhere—below or to the side?—he can hear Zamora bellowing his name.

"Major?" he shouts and hurries his feet, doing his best not to stumble and fall.

He rounds a corner—and comes face-to-face with La Loca.

Her coat is now black, but he recognizes her at once. And, with a shiver, he recognizes the ragged, awful laughter that's spilling from her mouth. For a second the laughter dies in her throat. She looks surprised—and then raises her gun, firing almost point-blank.

The explosion is loud—very loud—and her reactions are fast. But Danny's are faster. He ducks, and the bullet strikes the stone. Even as the ricochet falls harmlessly away, he turns and sprints back up the stairway.

"I've got you, Woo," La Loca chokes, the laughter whinnying up into her mouth as she chases after him. "I'm going to ki-kill you."

Danny climbs as fast as he can, stumbling now and then, hands shooting out to steady himself on the wall. She's not catching him but keeping pace. And every now and then, glancing back, he can see the gloved hand raise the gun and fire.

Bang. Another miss.

Another. *But that one was close*, he thinks. *Faster or she's going to get you.*

His legs are sagging under the effort now—and goodness knows how many hours without food or drink, and the effects of the drug . . .

Another door. He bundles through it rather than keep the effort of climbing—and finds himself facing the jumble of scaffolding rammed to the side of the Sagrada.

Perhaps I can lose her out there.

He starts to work his way out, as quickly as he dares, onto the bars of the orange tubing—a long, long drop opening up below his feet, the wind and darkness and exposure suddenly huge around him.

Another gunshot.

La Loca stands framed in the doorway, her gun raised. He flinches—but the bullet's already struck the scaffolding, deflecting away with a metallic twang.

She starts to work her way out after him, laughing like anything, hands working quickly as she swings through the scaffold, closing the gap.

And then, beyond—framed in the same doorway, he sees two more figures. It's Darko and Sing Sing. And then Aki beyond them.

"Stop!" Darko yells. "Leave him alone!"

"Keep going, Danny," his half sister shouts. "You're faster than her."

But he's not sure that he is. Perhaps a new strategy is needed. If the woman gets close enough then there won't be scaffolding to shield him from the bullets.

Ahead of him is the mighty trunk of one of the Sagrada's cranes. Up its core runs a caged ladder.

Climb down maybe? Faster than going monkey-like through the web of scaffold.

But as he clambers into the tube of the ladder he sees that a safety door is padlocked shut beneath his feet. The anti-climb spikes jagging out from the crane's side mean he can't climb around it. No lock pick to do the padlock.

So climb, then—some primal notion taking hold: the idea that you climb up to get to safety, rung after rung in his hand and then gone, the drop below growing with every step.

La Loca is below him now, on the ladder—about thirty feet below, trying to steady her laughter and aim, balancing the gun on the crook of her arm. Danny climbs on frantically—steeling for the gunshot— passing through another trapdoor. He moves quickly through it, banging the metal plate shut behind him, just as the gun fires. It shudders as the bullet hits.

Too close—got to keep climbing.

He's picturing the operator's cabin now, the one he saw from Javier's flat: that little bubble of calm and serenity floating over the city. *Maybe I can be safe there*, he thinks, vaguely aware that he's not really thinking straight. Maybe the effects of the drug still drag at his synapses.

Higher and higher.

The city falls away—even the might of the Sagrada dropping below him. Climbing up past that big glowing word, *HOSANNA*.

One hand after another, one rung after another. Exhaustion reaching up to grab him.

When he looks down he can see La Loca not fifteen feet behind. Almost past caring, he pauses, waits for the gunshot.

OK, just do it, he thinks. *The hanged man came true. So now comes death. Maybe that's OK . . .*

La Loca holds back her laughter long enough to take aim—and then, in the hush that follows, the click is quite audible. Another click as the striking pin hits an empty chamber. And then the laughter takes hold of her again.

Out of ammunition.

And below, Darko and Sing Sing and Aki are climbing fast, closing the gap.

The woman screams now, a horrific guttural scream that goes echoing away over the towers of the cathedral. She hurls the empty gun down at her chasers and then pulls a long shard of a knife from her boot, clamping it between her teeth, coming up the ladder again like lightning.

There's nothing above now but the cabin of the crane. The ground, hundreds of feet below, the wind and the drop tugging at him.

Danny reaches the door of the darkened booth.

If I can just get in there and shut the door, then I can rest. Close my eyes. Sleep.

But it's locked.

La Loca is so close he can hear her breathing between the bouts of demented laughter.

Where now?

He looks along the boom arm, hanging skeletal over the park far below. Maybe she won't dare to follow.

There's no choice, so he starts out across the void, hands gripping the cold metal, feet striding from one rib to the next. He looks back. She's still coming. Determined—or crazy. His energy is slipping away and she's closing fast.

It's no good . . .

And she's stooping to grab his shoulder in a vise-like grip, snaring him, holding the knife high, ready to strike, her face suddenly calm, as if the storm has blown away.

"*Adéu,*" she says, taking careful aim.

And then her expression changes, struck suddenly,

it seems, by a dramatic change of mind. The laughter dies. Her arm drops slowly to her side, her face losing power, surprised, then blank, her head leaning to one side. And without another sound, her eyes closing, she lurches over to her right, spinning, exposing the knife that has hit her in the back of the neck, its handle familiar . . .

She stumbles against the framework, reaches for a grip on nothing, and falls, lifelessly, into the abyss. Her coat flaring like giant wings as she falls, exposing for a second its violent green lining as she plummets into the park below.

Danny looks away. Hears her body crash through the canopy of the trees, sending parakeets screeching from their roosts.

He slumps against the frame of the jib, clinging onto it for dear life, suddenly feeling very exposed, desperate to hold onto life.

Behind him he hears a voice—Sing Sing's— bright, dancing with energy again.

"What a flipping shot, Darko! You got her!"

Danny looks back and sees the knife thrower fixed in his post-throw stance. Darko's breathing hard, fighting to hold onto his fabled composure, looking at his outstretched throwing hand as if unsure that what's just happened is real. His eyes travel to the black drop below, and he shakes his head once and closes his eyes.

"You reap just what you sow," he growls.

But Sing Sing is already coming steadily along the boom, her face bright with the effort of the chase, the relief, the shock of the last few minutes.

"You're OK!" she's saying. "I thought I'd lost you!"

Danny nods, but his mind's trying to come to terms with what has just happened. What it all means. The crane vibrates as the wind gusts again.

La Loca is gone. Maybe another piece of the threat gone with her. But another piece of the puzzle too.

Maybe she could have told me something more. Maybe she could have told me about Jimmy—or why Mum and Dad had to die in the fire. Why the Forty-Nine want ME dead.

He gets to his knees, steadying himself on the handrail, the wind ruffling his hair.

But at least he knows where to go next. He needs to ask Rosa everything she knows—demand she be honest with him, completely honest—and then he needs to head for a confrontation with Jimmy T. And maybe the next two codes will tell him more of what he needs to know. Will open the mystery even wider.

He looks at the lights shining on the crazy towers of the Sagrada, the other cranes glowing yellow, luminous against the vast darkened city beyond. The sea shimmering.

The moon above it all.

He gets to his feet and turns to Sing Sing, a point of light sparking each eye. Oblivious now to the drop below.

"Did you see me?" he says quietly, to her, to himself—to the others who can no longer hear him.

"Did you see me?" he shouts. "I did it! I'm still here." And he starts to make his way back to safety, toward his sister.

ACKNOWLEDGMENTS

Thanks to my eternally supportive agent, Kirsty McLachlan at DGA—and to my wonderfully perceptive editor, Jon Appleton, and the rest of the team at Hodder Children's Books. Their help and support is much appreciated.

Thanks again to Isabel (crack that code!), Marcus—and to Thomas Taylor for his constant encouragement.

And special thanks to my two boys: Will, for supplying a key idea to drive the plot in the preceding pages—and Joe, for (literally) picking me off the floor when a hard drive meltdown led to thirty thousand un-backed-up words of *The Palace of Memory* evaporating into the ether one rainy November day. Couldn't have done this without the help of you both.

ABOUT THE AUTHOR

Julian Sedgwick is an author of children's books who lives in England with his wife and two sons. Julian's lifelong interest in the arts and culture of China and Japan has influenced much of his work, as has his fascination with performance, street art, and the circus.